The Callahan Cousins

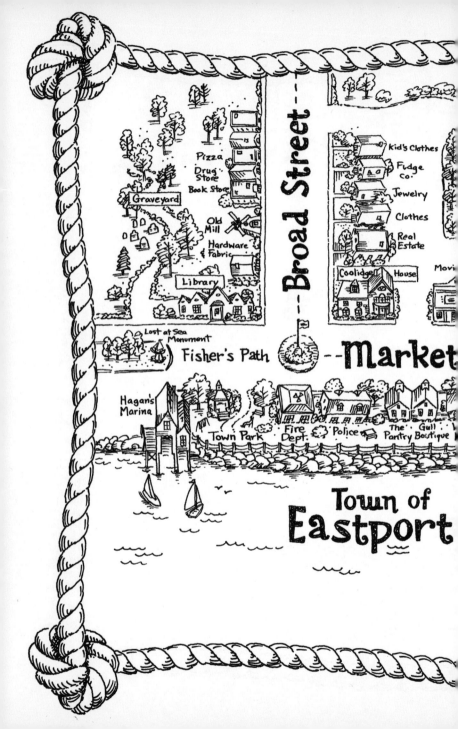

Callahan Cousins

Together Again
by Elizabeth Doyle Carey

LITTLE, BROWN AND COMPANY

New York ↝ Boston

Little, Brown and Company

Hachette Book Group USA
1271 Avenue of the Americas, New York, NY 10020
Visit our Web site at www.lb-kids.com

First Edition: October 2006

ISBN-13: 978-0-316-73695-4
ISBN-10: 0-316-73695-3

10   9   8   7   6   5   4   3   2   1

Q-MT

Printed in the United States of America

Book design by Alyssa Morris

The text was set in Mrs. Eaves and the display was set in Bickley Script

Don't miss these other great
Callahan Cousins adventures:
Summer Begins
Home Sweet Home
Keeping Cool

For Liam, Finn, and Niall: Brothers forever!

And for Alex, with a million kisses.

—

Special thanks to Jennifer Hunt and Rebekah McKay.

The Callahan Cousins

"Send them to me," said grandma Gee.
And so they did.

Proper Christmas

$\mathcal{T}$he interior of the ferry's cabin was stuffy and smelled strongly of popcorn grease from the snack bar and diesel fuel. Silver tinsel was strewn here and there, with some tacked-up cardboard cutouts of Christmas trees and menorahs. Outside, the wind was frigid and gusty and the water of the sound choppy, with small waves whacking the sides of the boat and splashing up on board in great gray sprays. They were drawing nearer to Gull Island, and Phoebe Callahan wanted to review the contents of the file she'd brought so that everything would be fresh in her mind and she could lay it all out clearly for her cousins tonight, when they had some privacy after dinner.

Phoebe withdrew the green folder from her hippie-style, knit, rainbow bag and placed it on the table in front of her. She neatly aligned the corners of the file with the edge of the table, then reached up and twisted her long, white blond hair into a bun. Next, she pushed up the sleeves of her knee-length, granny-style wool cardigan (Phoebe believed that old-fashioned clothes were superior in construction and style to modern ones), crossed her long, long legs in their heavy painter's pants, opened her file, and leaned back against the slippery vinyl seat of the booth. Luckily, the ferry was nearly empty and she had the booth all to herself, or she would have felt self-conscious about the file's contents (Phoebe was a very private person; formal, almost, and she believed in keeping oneself to oneself). Instead, she allowed the file to flop open generously, and she took her time looking at it, sighing quietly as she perused its contents. Her hand rested on the tab with the file's title; "Proper Christmas" the tab said.

Inside were colorful pages neatly slit from magazines, carefully typed lists and charts, handwritten recipes, lists of web addresses and links, plus written scenes Xeroxed from novels, with their corresponding illustrations copied, too. There was a whole chunk of articles carefully razored from newsprint, and printouts from microfiche, and photocopied pages of research books, highlighted in places with a green highlighter. Phoebe looked longingly at the collected images as she shuffled through the sheaves of paper. She sighed contentedly, allowing her imagination to drift. Her mouth watered as she conjured the various dishes described in her collected recipes, and her shoulders gave an involuntary shiver as she imagined the wonderful things in store for her and her cousins this Christmas on Gull.

After spending the whole summer on Gull Island without

any parents — with only their grandmother Gee and her Irish housekeeper, Sheila, to look after them — it had been very difficult for the four same-age cousins to part ways. The freedom they'd enjoyed, not to mention the adventures they'd had and the bonding they'd experienced, had been very hard to give up, and upon returning home in September, they'd all stayed deeply involved in each other's lives via daily e-mails. The idea of not seeing each other for months was unthinkable.

Phoebe had also missed being at Gee's sprawling seaside mansion, The Sound, because it was steeped in tradition and family history; and she'd missed New England, with its quaint appearance, antique houses, and authentic old-fashioned things like traffic rotaries and windmills and ice cream parlors. Phoebe loved history and the past, and leaving Gull Island meant returning to Florida, which was all about the new and the temporary and, in her mind, the ugly: ranch houses, shopping malls, highways that cut through beautiful natural scenery, and rootless people with no ties to Florida's past (what there was of it).

Phoebe had always been a fish out of water in Florida. Despite the fact that her appearance was quintessential beach girl — white blond hair, ever-tan skin, tall, thin, blue-eyed — she was really more of an indoor person. She loved to read — in particular historical fiction or eighteenth- and nineteenth-century novels — and she often imagined she had simply been born at the wrong time and in the wrong place, and maybe even to the wrong family. Her parents and her older and younger sisters (Melody was eight and Daphne was sixteen) were all about progress. They loved technology and modern furniture and new music and plastic gizmos; it all horrified Phoebe. Sometimes now, she exaggerated her horror to amuse them and they, too, exaggerated their loathing of "old" stuff and the past just to tease her. But when it came to Christmas, Phoebe was serious.

Growing up in Florida, Phoebe had never had what she considered a "real" Christmas. Christmases there were temperate, even warm, for starters, and kind of lonely, because most of her friends went away to cold places for the holidays. There were fake Christmas trees smothered in plastic angel decorations, and tinseled strip malls instead of quaintly decorated village squares, and no one wanted to eat roast beef and Yorkshire pudding for dinner when it was seventy degrees outside. In addition, her family — though nominally Catholic — wasn't very religious, so they didn't have any kind of a religious tradition either. And of course, she'd never had a white Christmas. So without any of the old-fashioned Christmas trappings and traditions, Phoebe felt that Christmases in Florida were lightweight, insubstantial, and brief.

As she grew older, Phoebe longed for the Christmases she'd read about in her favorite books — books like *Little House in the Big Woods, Little House on the Prairie,* and *Anne of Green Gables.* She wanted snowmen with carrot noses, horse-drawn sleighs with jingling bells, hot mulled cider, Christmas morning pancakes with real maple syrup, and a crackling fire blazing in the fire-place. She wanted to creep downstairs Christmas morning in a warm flannel nightgown, with feet like ice, to peek in at Santa's offerings under a huge, *real* Christmas tree . . . the works. She wanted to really *feel* Christmas.

So, in the beginning of November, when her cousin Neeve had floated the Christmas vacation idea in an e-mail with the subject header: "Xmas @ G's?" Phoebe had responded with enthusiasm. In fact, as soon as she'd received the e-mail, she'd rushed to grap her Proper Christmas folder from one of the filing cabinets in her bedroom. (Her room at home was as neat as a pin, with every book in its place on the alphabetized shelves, and every paper in its file in a filing cabinet.) She hadn't looked at the file's contents in a while — her Christmas fasci-nation had started three years ago and had really reached its peak about a year ago, but Phoebe still had the same feelings. *Finally!* she thought. *A dream come true!* And then, *I am not going to blow what might be my only chance for a perfect, old-fashioned, New England Christmas.*

She knew that her expectations were high, and her plans were specific. But each of the cousins — Neeve, Hillary, and Kate — would have a role that suited her personality and in-terests, and Phoebe was counting on them to help her make this her best Christmas ever: the Christmas she'd always dreamed about.

And now, she'd nearly arrived. Her booth was right next to the window, with a good view of their destination. Just off the coast of Rhode Island, Gull was a barrier island about an hour and half from the mainland by car ferry. It was shaped like a seagull in midflight, its wings outstretched, and it ran at an angle to the mainland, in an almost exact North/South orientation. The northern part of the island was known as North Wing, and it was where the summer residents had their large vacation homes (The Sound was there, even though Gee had recently moved there year-round). The southern end was called South Wing, and was home to Eastport Harbor, the island's only town.

As the ferry drew closer, Phoebe pressed her forehead against the cold glass to get a better look at the nearing island, and she couldn't believe that she was looking at the same Gull Island she'd left just four months earlier. All its summery greens had gone brown and gray, and the trees were stripped bare of leaves. The island looked harsh and uninhabitable in its present state — nothing like the inviting oasis that rose, fresh and inviting, out of the brilliant blue sound in the summertime. Phoebe, who had never visited it before in the wintertime, was thrilled. It was just what she'd hoped for — minus the snow. But that could still come. As she stared, Phoebe tried repeatedly to swallow the smile that kept blooming, unbidden, on her face; she was worried people might think she was crazy, sitting all alone, smiling to herself, but her anticipation and excitement kept causing the smile to return.

Chapter Two

Perfect

As the ferry bumped its way into its berth in Eastport Harbor, Phoebe quickly stowed the file, zipped her coat, donned her hat and mittens, and went to stand near the door, tossing her empty hot chocolate cup in the trash as she passed. The instant the deckhands finally waved everyone out and onto the deck, Phoebe began looking for the cousins and Gee, and it didn't take more than a second to spot them.

Neeve was wearing a reflective silver down jacket that was so shiny it looked like it could harness enough solar power to heat Gee's whole house, and Kate was shrieking Phoebe's name, while Hillary bounced athletically on the balls of her toes as if trying to keep warm. Gee had on a funny hat with big ear flaps hanging down from it, and her Volvo was parked askew in the strangely empty lot, the engine still running. Gee waved enthusiastically, and Phoebe finally allowed her smile free reign; she waved back, beaming, and strode to meet them, the wheels on her suitcase going *clickety-clack* when she crossed the dock.

Phoebe's usual formality was overcome by her joy at seeing the others. So there were huge, puffy hugs, and laughter, and everyone chattering all at once, and it was lovely to be back. Neeve had grown her hair out, and Kate had chopped hers even shorter, Hillary looked thinner, and Gee looked the same as always, except for the funny hat. They completely swarmed her, with Hillary grappling Phoebe's suitcase and swinging it into the trunk of the car, Neeve dragging her into the backseat, where the four of them crammed in all together, and Kate chattering like a magpie all the while. Gee smiled indulgently at them and climbed into the driver's seat.

Although it was only four o'clock, the sun was already sinking — earlier than it did in Florida at this time of year — and the afternoon was growing dusky around the edges.

Gee buckled up and they were off.

"We're going to get a tree, right now!" crowed Neeve.

Gee looked in the rearview mirror and smiled at Phoebe. "I wanted to wait to go to the tree lot until you'd all arrived. I think it's much more fun to do tree-trimming together, don't you?"

Phoebe's heart sank a little. One of her plans had been to go out in the woods and chop down a tree of their own, and she hated to be thwarted so early in her Christmas campaign. However, she knew, deep down inside, that the tree-chopping was not a realistic goal. For one thing, there really weren't any real woods on Gull, just a few treed areas here and there; and she still wasn't quite sure who she had in mind to swing the axe or saw the saw or whatever it was you had to do. It was sure to be hard. And she certainly hadn't thought about who would drag the heavy tree back to the house. Still. A fantasy was a fantasy.

But not wanting to disappoint Gee, who was looking at her expectantly, Phoebe lifted her chin, smiled, and replied, "Absolutely. At home, we always decorate our tree the night that we get out for Christmas vacation. My mother makes Swedish cinnamon buns and my father gets out all the boxes of ornaments, and everyone participates." Phoebe nodded for emphasis. She knew she'd made her family Christmas sound somewhat traditional, but that was about the only traditional thing they did. The rest of their holiday behavior drove her crazy. In fact, right before she'd left, they'd been debating buying an artificial tree for this year. Awful! Phoebe nearly shuddered just thinking about it now.

"That's when we do our tree, too!" said Kate. "Except every year we do a different theme for the tree, so some years my mom and I will make dozens of gingerbread angels to hang, or one year we did all flowers, just white ones, in little bud holders, with only white lights. . . ."

"Easy there, Martha Stewart," said Neeve. She turned to Phoebe, "Is she drooling? Seriously. I'm just checking, because I don't want her to ruin Gee's car." Kate punched Neeve, and Neeve cried out and rubbed her arm.

"You think you're so funny. I'd like to see you try making your own ornaments, hot stuff!" But Kate was only pretending to be mad.

"*Hot stuff?*" said Hillary incredulously, turning in her seat. "Where did you get that expression? The 1970s?"

Phoebe smiled in quiet amusement, but she was quickly distracted by the sights of town passing by her window, and she craned her neck to drink it all in. Along Market Street, the touristy junk stores were closed for the season, but everywhere else was decked out with holiday decorations: cottony "snow" was pillowed inside shop windows, pinecone garlands were looped here and there, a few cheerful menorahs twinkled, and fresh green wreaths hung robustly on every door. The town had put potted Christmas trees in a long row down each sidewalk, and they were lit with colorful bulbs, and a big red bow was suspended over the road, hung from wires attached high in the air to buildings on either side of the street. The movie theater was showing *It's a Wonderful Life* as well as the new action blockbuster film of the season, and even the flagpole in the middle of the roundabout had been wrapped with an evergreen garland. It was all tasteful and New Englandy, and just what she'd hoped for. But even more than the decorations, Phoebe was pleased by the stark winter landscape, the bare black branches against the darkening sky, the cold air seeping in around the car door, and people bustling along in scarves and hats and mittens.

"So this is Christmas in New England," Phoebe narrated.

"Do you like it so far?" Gee asked, her eyes twinkling in the rearview mirror.

"It's certainly different than a crèche under a palm tree," said Phoebe drily. Her disdain for tropical Christmas traditions was endless, and she could handily mask her excitement with it. She wasn't quite ready to show her wild hopes and feelings to everyone, private as she was. She continued, "But it's wonderful so far. The cold surprised me, but the rest of it is just what I've always read about." *And wished for,* she added to herself.

Kate turned to Phoebe with interest. "That's right! What do you think of the weather?"

"Obviously, I've been to cold places before. I mean, I was even in Sweden one December for Santa Lucia day when I was little, but it's been a while. I'd forgotten how bracing it is. . . ."

Kate smiled, her cheeks rosy, and her nose running a tiny bit. She gave Phoebe's knee a little squeeze of enthusiasm. "If bracing means good, then I agree. I love it. It's my favorite time of year."

Phoebe smiled. "Bracing means cold." Her vocabulary often stumped the cousins.

Hillary snorted from the front seat. "The reason you love the winter, Kate, is because you don't have to go outside. You can just stay indoors for hours on end!"

Kate was a real homebody, it was true.

Neeve laughed and clapped her hands at Hillary's observation. "Totally! Good call!"

Kate rolled her eyes at them. "You'll love it, too, Bee. You'll see. It just takes a day or two to get used to the weather, and then it's really fun. . . ."

Little did Kate know that Phoebe didn't need any convincing. But before Kate could go on, Phoebe interrupted her with a sharp intake of breath. "Oh! Look at the library!" The library was all aglow with white holiday lights trimming every window, door, and eve. It was as if someone had taken a bright highlighter and illuminated only the outlines of the building; with the darkening of the day, it seemed to float like magic in the air.

"Isn't that wonderful?" said Gee. "They started that about two years ago and it's already become a great tradition."

"They did something like that to the Old Mill, too. Look back . . . ," said Kate, gesturing to her favorite store on the island.

Phoebe craned her neck to see over the backseat and caught a glimpse of the spokes of the windmill, all lit up with rows of white lights. She turned forward again and was rewarded by the sight of a huge tree on the town green — how had she never realized before that the giant tree growing there was a *Christmas tree*? — strung with blue lights, with a giant white star on top and a big menorah planted in the ground right next to it.

"*Perfect!*" she breathed quietly. And then, louder, "Where do we go for our tree?" she asked.

"Cabot's. In the parking lot," said Neeve knowledgeably. "It's a charity thing, right, Gee? For . . ."

"The profit all goes to the animal shelter on the mainland," explained Gee.

"That's sweet," said Phoebe. Part of her agenda for this vacation was doing charitable things, and this would definitely count. She was a big dog-and-cat lover anyway.

And then they were there, Gee smoothly turning the car into the lot, and the girls all clambering out. The smell of pine was instant and all-encompassing. "Mmmm!" breathed Phoebe, and when she spoke her breath came out in great clouds in the air. "Hey! Look!" she laughed. "I forgot!" She breathed out heavily, over and over, marveling at the white smoke.

"That you can see your breath? Yeah. It's cool, isn't it?" agreed Hillary.

Gee was moving swiftly ahead, greeting the volunteers who stood around the propane outdoor heater, accepting a Styrofoam cup of something warm to drink, and laughing sociably. "Yoo-hoo! Girls!" she called them over with a wave of her mittened hand. "Look who I've found!"

Phoebe walked over, peering at the heavily dressed figures to see if she recognized anyone under their hats. It wasn't until she was right up close and heard their voices that she realized it was Smitty, who ran the boat repair shop down on the docks, and Mr. Saint John, the cousins' friend Talbot's dad, and the church pastor, Father Ryan, who looked most un-priest-like in his huge L.L. Bean down coat and pom-pom ski hat.

The girls all greeted the adults and accepted cups of cocoa

from the big drum of it nearby, and while Neeve grilled Mr. Saint John on Talbot's whereabouts, Phoebe strolled into the rows of trees that leaned heavily against the temporary lumber racks that had been constructed to support them. The trees in the front were short and fat, and Phoebe had no use for them. They felt like amateur trees, or trees for people living in condos in Miami, not family homestead Christmas trees. No. If this was going to be the Christmas she'd always dreamed of, they would need a major tree.

Phoebe pushed on and was rewarded for her perseverance toward the back of the lot, where the trees towered over her, dwarfing her like she was a tiny child again. She inhaled the pine scent, and closed her eyes, allowing her imagination to drift back to the clippings from her file. Should this be an all-white Victorian tree, with lace bows and white lights and only glass ornaments? Or a natural tree, with popcorn and cranberry garlands, pinecones, and . . .

"Bee!" Phoebe's eyes snapped open and she smiled, her fictional world replaced by an equally good real one. "Back here!" she replied, and was quickly rewarded with the sight of the three cousins bustling single file through the row of trees.

"We think we've found one," said Kate.

"Already?" Phoebe asked. She realized she had her hand on the trunk of one of the large trees and she self-consciously withdrew it. If everyone else was going to be happy with a smaller tree up front, she didn't want to be the one to ask Gee for a huge tree. No matter how great it would be, she couldn't be greedy. At least not all on her own.

But Hillary was distracted by the huge trees. "Hey, what about one of these?" she asked. She grabbed one and gave it a shake. Phoebe's heart leapt in hope, but she said nothing.

"Careful!" said Kate in alarm. "What if it falls over?"

"They're trees, Kate. It's not, 'you break it, you buy it,'" laughed Neeve.

Casually, Phoebe asked, "What *do* you think of this one?" She gestured to the tree she'd just had her hand on. She didn't want to appear too desperate; she wanted the others to just want the same one. It would be better that way.

"Oh . . . ," said Neeve, looking up at the great tall tree.

"Girls!" Suddenly they could hear Gee, and they called out in response until she rounded the corner and found them. "Oh my!" she said, looking up at the tall trees admiringly.

"We thought we'd found one up front," explained Hillary, "but then Phoebe had picked these, which we think are a lot better."

Phoebe blushed, and glanced sideways at Hillary. She was half-relieved that Hillary had figured out what she wanted, and half-annoyed at Hillary for announcing it. She looked back and up at the tree to hide the blush on her cheeks. Everyone else looked at Gee expectantly.

"I think they're gorgeous," said Gee, tipping her head back to get a good look.

Phoebe held her breath, hoping.

"Just right," said Gee, tapping her gloved finger on her chin. "Yes."

Phoebe sighed a huge sigh of relief and turned to smile at Gee, and Gee winked back at her. Phoebe was suddenly mortified. Was it that obvious that she'd wanted a big one so badly? She was acutely conscious of the fact that she didn't want Gee to know about her file and all of her deep Christmas desires. She didn't want Gee to think she was just using her and that this vacation was all about getting what *she* wanted. Because it wasn't. Really.

Gee tried to pull it off the rack to get a sense of its full height, but it was too heavy. "I think we'll need one of the gentlemen to help us," Gee said.

"I'll go get someone," offered Hillary, and she jogged off. Moments later, Smitty was with them, hoisting the tree to its feet, so to speak, and teasing them all.

"Going to make granny go for the big one this year, huh, kiddies?" Even though he was short in stature, he was strong, so he spun the tree easily in his hand and pushed down the branches like a salesman. "This is a good one. Lots of spring to it, fresh . . . ," he said as he rolled a small twig between his gloved thumb and finger to show that none of the needles were falling off. "A statement tree. The Rolls-Royce of the bunch." He winked. "And it should only take you about a week to decorate it."

Gee looked at the girls. "Happy?" she asked.

"Oh *yes!*" said Phoebe fervently, and when the others laughed at her uncharacteristic display of emotion, she ducked her chin.

Gee studied the tree appraisingly for another moment, and then said, "Can you deliver it in someone's truck, though? I don't think there's any way we could manage it on our own."

"Sure thing, Mrs. C. Jack will bring it over in the morning and set it up for you. Have you got a big stand to handle it? Cause this isn't a sissy tree. This one needs a nice big base."

Gee nodded. "I have just the thing. Thanks, Smitty. You're a dear." And the Callahans all filed back up front to pay for the tree.

Phoebe took a last glance over her shoulder at the tree. "See you tomorrow," she whispered, and she jammed her hands deep into her pockets and strolled away with a bounce in her step.

CHAPTER THREE

An Announcement

$\mathcal{B}$y now it was dark, and the drive home across the causeway was unremarkable, because there was nothing that could be lit up in holiday fashion along the way. Once they reached North Wing, one or two houses had tastefully strung some lights on their trees or bushes, but, as Gee explained, not a lot of summer people came out to Gull in the wintertime. In fact, many of her neighbors closed down their houses Labor Day weekend, turning off the water, even boarding up windows, until the following Memorial Day.

Phoebe was quiet now, quieter than usual even. All of her attention was focused on her avid wish that The Sound, Gee's mammoth and gorgeous house, lived up to her hopes and expectations of a perfect New England Christmas. And if it didn't, she had to figure out — politely — how to make it so it did.

And then they were there, turning up the driveway,

crunching over the crushed, now frozen, seashells that paved it. Phoebe craned her neck to get a glimpse as soon as possible. Up ahead, Gee's big white house stood on a rise, three stories tall, with wings reaching out from either side in a welcoming embrace. It was dark now, so the yard wasn't really visible, but the house was all lit up.

"Wow!" breathed Phoebe in a mixture of awe and relief, for in every window — and there were a lot of them — burned a small, cozy, electric candle. *This is definitely a good start,* she thought.

"Sheila did that last week," said Gee. "Quite a project, finding them all, replacing bulbs, laying out the extension cords. It looks so pretty, but I just don't have the patience for it, myself."

They pulled into the small parking area in front of the house. "It was worth it," said Phoebe quietly, looking up through the car window. On the front door was a huge green wreath, with a red plaid ribbon flapping gaily in the breeze, and Phoebe could smell delicious wood smoke from someone's chimney. They never had fires in Florida — her house didn't even have a fireplace — so most of her exposure to fireplaces had been through books or movies and the occasional visit to her cousins' houses or to Sweden. *Already, this is really good,* thought Phoebe. She hardly dared to hope for more.

The wind had grown stronger, and the other girls hustled inside as Gee helped Phoebe with her bag. Glancing up,

Phoebe took in the view of icy-looking stars beginning to twinkle against the clear black sky.

"Will it snow while we're here, do you think?" she asked Gee, as they crunched across the driveway.

"Funny you should mention it, sweetheart. I think we might be due for a dusting tomorrow. But bear in mind that when we do get snow, it usually doesn't stick. Besides the fact that it blows away so quickly, the salt melts it. Snow on Gull is usually fleeting. Anyway, even if we do get snow tonight, we're due for an unseasonably warm snap this week, I believe." Gee reached for the brass handle to open the front door, and Phoebe followed her. She conveniently blocked out what Gee had said about the warm front coming and focused instead on the snow. *A dusting is a good start,* thought Phoebe. It was more than she'd ever had back home, and with a white Christmas as one of her primary goals this year, this was great news.

To Phoebe's pleasant surprise, the house inside was totally changed. There were heavy oriental rugs down on the slate floor of the front hall, where in the summer it had been cool and bare. The banister on the front stairs was wrapped in a long evergreen garland that smelled wonderful, and on the tall front hall table, giant glass hurricane lamps held dried cranberries with huge cream-colored candles nestled inside, and a huge pot of tall, splashy red amaryllis sat in between them. Phoebe glanced to her left into the living room, where logs were laid in the fireplace and low bowls of paperwhites bloomed fragrantly, and was stunned to see all the furniture slipcovered in scarlet-colored flannel. Big brocade throw pillows were scattered around, and two furry fake mink blankets were draped on the backs of the couches, and a fluffy cream-colored sheepskin rug lay in front of the fireplace. This was even better than she'd hoped!

"Gee!" she sputtered in surprise. "What happened? It looks like a Brontë novel in here!"

Gee laughed. "I should've warned you for the surprise, after how the others reacted. It's just the house's winter warm-up. Sheila and I change everything over in October every year — putting down cozy rugs, and changing the slipcovers on the furniture from the white duck to flannel. It gets too chilly in here otherwise. I'm sorry it caught you off guard, dear. There are a few changes in the kitchen, too, but nothing dramatic. You see, the truth is, I always wanted a red living room, but it just didn't seem right for a summer house. But then, when I started staying here year-round, I thought, well . . ."

"Oh, I *adore* it!" insisted Phoebe, drinking everything in. Aside from adding the tree and maybe one or two more holiday decorations, there wouldn't be much for Phoebe to do to get things in line with her fantasies.

They meandered companionably down the hall to the kitchen where the other girls' voices already floated above the sound of Christmas carols playing from the kitchen radio. A wonderful smell of cinnamon plus something heartier beckoned Phoebe.

She entered the kitchen and was met by more changes. A small fire leapt and danced in the brick kitchen fireplace, and a heavy white bed quilt covered the kitchen table as a tablecloth. The pale green cushions of the banquette had been slip-covered in dark green plaid flannel, and there was a sprig of mistletoe jauntily tacked to the wall above the windows. Another thick oriental rug covered the wood floor, and at the back door, a huge, bottle-green velvet curtain had been hung to protect from drafts. There were bowls of bright fruit everywhere — clementines, oranges, lemons, and a big bowl of walnuts presided over by an old-fashioned nutcracker in the shape of a soldier with a long white beard. A miniature potted Christmas tree stood on the sideboard like a sentry. And at the stove, stirring a big crock of some sort of fragrant stew, was Sheila, Gee's longtime Irish cook and housekeeper. Petite, and whippet-thin as ever, she was probably as old as Gee but never seemed to age.

"Hi, Sheila," said Phoebe shyly.

"Welcome back, luv! Happy Christmas," said Sheila, wiping her hands on the red and green Christmas apron she'd cinched around her tiny waist. Phoebe was reserved and self-contained; so she didn't throw herself at Sheila for a hug or anything, like the others probably had. Sheila reached for Phoebe's hand and gave it a firm squeeze with both of hers, which felt just right, as far as Phoebe was concerned. "It's wonderful to see you, you look like the picture of health with that tan of yours at this time of year." Sheila cocked her head appreciatively, not a hair out of place on her neat, gray head.

"Thanks. It's great to see you, too. Merry Christmas, almost. What are you cooking?" Phoebe crossed the room to check, circling the butcher block island.

"It's a *coq au vin,* chicken with . . ."

". . . wine sauce!" finished Phoebe. "Yum."

"And there are some mashed potatoes, with an apple cinnamon crumble for dessert. It'll warm your bones."

A crystal bowl stood on the counter, ready to receive the stew, and a beautiful bone china bowl with a holly border looked as if it was for the mashed potatoes. Everything was festive and beautifully decorative, and Phoebe was excited.

"It all sounds delicious! I feel like I've walked into the pages of *A Christmas Carol.*"

"Speaking of which," interrupted Neeve from across the room, where she was trying on different hats and scarves and checking out the results in the mirror by the back door. "Talbot's dad said a lot of kids are going caroling one night this week. Talbot and some of his friends are organizing it. We should go." Neeve wasn't a great singer, but she loved to socialize, and Kate was eager to go, and Hillary would do anything that involved being outside in the fresh air. Now Neeve wrapped herself in some kind of tie-dyed pashmina and came to sit at the table with Kate.

Kate looked up from the magazine she was reading at the table and smiled.

"Perfect!" said Phoebe. Things were already dovetailing so nicely with her Christmas plans, and she hadn't even had a chance to spell it all out for the others yet.

"Oh, girls, I have a treat for you, too!" added Gee, with a sparkle in her eye. "I'd been waiting until you were all here to tell you, so now I can."

"What? What is it?" clamored the girls. Hillary turned from where she was warming her hands by the fire and came to sit. Gee's treats were always good ones. Even Sheila turned from the stove with a smile to hear what Gee had up her sleeve.

Phoebe joined the others at the table, and slid her long legs along the banquette and into the warm folds of the quilt tablecloth. While she waited, she twisted her long hair into a new bun, and then reached for a clementine to peel and eat. Splitting the rind with her fingernails, she peeled it quickly and the strong orange aroma joined the other delicious smells that were perfuming the kitchen. She licked the dribbling juice from her knuckle and began to eat.

Meanwhile, everyone was looking at Gee expectantly, while she crossed to her kitchen desk and withdrew a sheet of pale green paper. She lifted her reading glasses from the chain around her neck and perched them on the end of her nose, then sat in her usual chair at the head of the kitchen table, crossing her legs.

Looking around at the girls, she smiled and said, "This is

something I picked up at The Nature Conservancy's silent auction a month ago, once I knew you were all returning for Christmas. I thought it might be a great adventure for you all, and I only wish I was young enough to participate myself." She looked down at the paper and read, "*'This coupon entitles the bearer to an old-fashioned Christmas sleepover for six at The Gull Island Whaling Museum, complete with historical tales, traditional Christmas crafts, snacks and drinks . . . ,'*" but she couldn't finish, her voice was so drowned out by shrieks.

Neeve was up, wheeling around the kitchen in glee. Hillary tipped back in her chair and pumped her fist in the air, shouting, "Yes! Yes! Yes!" and Kate's face turned bright pink with emotion.

But Phoebe positively glowed with joy. Besides the fact that this would give her the chance to really experience a traditional New England Christmas, one of her all-time favorite books was *From the Mixed-up Files of Mrs. Basil E. Frankweiler,* in which a brother and sister move into the Metropolitan Museum of Art in New York City. Sleeping in a museum was one of Phoebe's fantasies of all time!

Inside, her heart was thumping with joy, but she smiled calmly at the others and waited patiently for them to quiet down. She wasn't one for big displays of emotion — it just felt inappropriate — tacky, even — to make a spectacle of oneself the way the others did. Neeve always went crazy over stuff, dancing and jumping, arms flailing; and Hillary cheered and whistled when she was pleased. Phoebe couldn't even cry or pout the way Kate did when she was sad — with huge glistening teardrops and an outturned lower lip. Phoebe told herself she was measured, thoughtful, and appropriate. The others teased her that she was closed off, repressed, uptight, even cold. She wasn't sure what was true. She just knew that *inside*, she felt the same as the others looked *outside*.

Wanting to participate in some way, however, Phoebe cleared her throat. "Ahem." Kate heard her and looked over at Phoebe with a question in her eyes. "Ahem!" said Phoebe again, loudly this time. She selected another clementine and began peeling it while she waited for the others' attention.

"What?" asked Neeve, mid-hip thrust. Hillary paused, too, and everyone looked at Phoebe. *"Jingle bell, jingle bell, jingle bell rock . . . ,"* went the radio.

"It says the party is for six guests," noted Phoebe, popping a section of orange into her mouth and chewing thoughtfully.

"Lark, obviously," said Neeve, mentioning their good friend from the summertime. She slid gracefully back into her seat and energetically drummed her fingers on the quilted tabletop.

Everyone seemed in agreement, so Phoebe said, "Okay. And number six?"

An unspoken name hung in the air like a storm cloud. They were all thinking it, but no one dared to utter it.

Sloan Bicket was their sometimes-friend and sometimes-enemy from this summer on Gull Island. She was the same age as the Callahan cousins and her father had also been a sometimes-friend, sometimes-enemy of all the Callahan girls' dads when *they* were growing up in the summers on Gull. The problem was, Sloan could be really evil. And Phoebe, in particular, couldn't stand her most of the time. But Lark was ostensibly her best friend, and Hillary had made peace with Sloan early in the summer; Neeve was sort of friendly with Sloan, in the way she was friendly with anyone she ever met, and toward the end of the summer, even Kate had gotten really buddy-buddy with her, much to Phoebe's chagrin. Phoebe flat-out hated Sloan.

And now, with the other three all such great pals of Sloan's, Phoebe knew that if they invited Lark, they'd have to invite Sloan. And Sloan would ruin it. But what really worried Phoebe was that it was three against one, and she needed them all on her side to fulfill her Christmas plans. She couldn't alienate them all over this. Blast! What was she going to do?

Everyone looked at each other uncomfortably, and then Hillary said, "For number six, how about Tessa? From sailing clinic?"

There was a brief silence while everyone mulled this over, but then no one jumped on the idea. "Or Andrea?" added Neeve half-heartedly.

"Guys, you know how much it would mean to her to be included," said Kate quietly. Everyone knew she wasn't talking about Tessa or Andrea.

"Oh, here we go, ruining our night before it's even begun," huffed Phoebe. She couldn't help herself! Sloan was just so evil!

Kate looked pleadingly at Phoebe. "Come on, Bee. . . . We've been through this before. . . ."

But Phoebe didn't have to answer, at least for now.

"Girls, the good thing is, you don't need to decide it right this minute," Gee interrupted brightly. "Thanks, Sheila," she said, gratefully accepting a mug of coffee. "Why don't I call the museum first thing tomorrow, get the details, and we'll pick a night. Then we can worry about who is or isn't going, *okay*?" The "okay" was heavily stressed because Gee didn't want the Sloan debate to continue in front of Sheila. Sheila was Sloan's half-aunt, and although there was no love lost between the two of them (Sheila generally referred to Sloan as "that brat" and Sloan called Sheila "the old goat"), Gee didn't like the girls to badmouth Sloan in front of her relative. From over by the stove, Sheila started whistling loudly along with the Christmas carols, to show that she wasn't listening.

"Okay," agreed Phoebe. There was no way Sloan was going to come along and ruin her once-in-a-lifetime chance at an amazing night after-hours in a museum, and a Christmassy one at that. She'd have to work on the others when they were alone later.

The two clementines had temporarily satisfied Phoebe's hunger, and now she wondered if she had time for a quick shower before dinner. She glanced at her watch. "Where are we staying?" During the summer, the girls had started out staying in the main house, but had transferred down to the

Dorm, the traditional teenagers' guest house at the foot of Gee's property.

"You're back in the main house, Phoebe, my dear. I hope it's okay with you. The Dorm isn't heated and I don't like the idea of you girls down there with space heaters." Gee wrinkled her nose at the thought.

Phoebe didn't mind. The Dorm was a summer-type of house anyway, like a surf shack. It wouldn't be very cozy at this time of year. "That's fine. So it's our former accommodations?" she asked formally, but with a smile to show she was joking.

"Yes."

"You're with me again, you lucky dog," said Hillary. "I haven't even had time to trash the place yet." Phoebe liked things to be neat, and Hillary's sloppiness could sometimes drive her crazy. Phoebe found neatness relaxing; when everything was in its place, it freed her mind to focus on other things.

"Hmm. I'll have to see about that. Your idea of trashing the place and mine are pretty different," Phoebe said with a sideways smile that showed Hillary she was just teasing.

Phoebe stood, dumped her orange peels in the trash, and went back to the front hall to claim her luggage. Then she bumped it up the sisal-covered front stairs and turned down the long hall to claim her room and produce her Christmas file. She couldn't wait to present it to the others tonight. But it would take some finesse, she could see now.

Chapter Four

Decorating

$\mathscr{T}$rue to her promise, Sheila's dinner was warming and delicious. The potatoes were creamy and rich, the chicken stew a nice, tangy counterpoint, and Sheila's winter salad of field greens, candied walnuts, blue cheese, and sliced pear was a tasty surprise — something Phoebe would never have tried under normal circumstances, but scrumptious. For dessert, Sheila gave them vanilla ice cream sprinkled liberally with coarsely chopped candy canes — a kind of spontaneous peppermint ice cream that tasted like Christmas itself. Grateful, the girls had tried to take over the kitchen cleanup, but Sheila had hustled them out, as usual, instructing them to instead lend a hand to their grandmother by bringing the tree ornaments and assorted other decorations down from the attic.

Although she was not a fan of clutter, like Neeve, nor was she artsy craftsy like Kate, Phoebe was thrilled about decorating for Christmas. She had all kinds of ideas in mind from her files, and she was pleased that Gee hadn't finished the process before they'd arrived (save for the flowers and the seasonal changeovers, of course). And she couldn't wait to basically do the opposite of every holiday thing her parents had ever done.

Except for their tree, which was pretty traditional, Phoebe's parents' notion of decorating for Christmas was very Spartan and lackadaisical, with no sense of tradition (even from year to year), nor history. One year her dad might bring home some goofy pink flamingoes with Santa hats on to stick in the front yard as kind of a joke; the next year her mom might buy a wreath made of seashells to hang on the door. It frustrated Phoebe to no end, which amused her parents, and irritated her older sister ("Why do you care?" Daphne would ask, in a pained voice. Phoebe's younger sister Melody didn't even notice). But Phoebe did care. Without family living nearby in Florida, and without a long family history there, and stuck in the temporary, disposable ambiance of their suburb, Phoebe felt rootless — like she could just float away and no one would ever notice. It was kind of scary.

Tonight, Phoebe was dying to see what Gee had in storage. After sixty-plus years of New England Christmases (and maybe more, if Gee had inherited stuff from her parents), there promised to be quite a collection of traditional — maybe even historical — stuff. Unlike Phoebe and her family, Gee was seriously rooted.

Gee had two attics, one at either end of the third floor.

They bracketed a suite of six "maids'" rooms, some of which belonged to Sheila. Inside the sloped-ceiling storage rooms were generations of semiorganized clutter which had been the finding ground for many elements of the décor of the Dorm that the girls had redecorated, as well as family keepsakes that had both inspired and enriched the girls' summer adventures.

Gee accompanied them upstairs, which was a first. Usually they explored the attics on their own. She directed them to the attic room at the south end of the house, and pointed out the shopping bags and boxes that contained ornaments, strings of lights, the crèche, and a few other elements. Naturally, she began trying to haul the stuff out herself, but the girls wouldn't hear of it. Their parents always instructed them not to let Gee work hard when they were around. So despite her laughing protests that she wasn't an old lady yet, the girls themselves hauled the supplies — about ten boxes and bags in all — down to the living room.

Then they all gathered around the pile to start sorting. By now it was getting late, nine o'clock or so, and Gee suggested it would be best to leave the ornaments in their boxes until the tree arrived anyway. Instead, Neeve pulled out lights from a shopping bag and untangled them while Gee explained that no matter how hard she and Sheila tried to put them away neatly, the lights seemed to get all jumbled on their own. Kate unpacked the crèche — a beautiful antique nativity scene that Gee had bought in Provence, France, many years ago, with figures about the size of Barbie dolls, carved of wood and carefully painted with gold leaf and incredible detailing. The donkey had real horsehair for its tail and mane, and the camels were furry, if a little threadbare. And there was even a small manger lined with a sheep's wool blanket for the little baby Jesus figurine. At the bottom of the packing box was a sturdy wooden shed that served as the barn. Kate set it all up on the long side table that Gee had suggested, and everyone came over to admire it.

Phoebe couldn't believe the craftsmanship of the set. It was more beautiful than any other holiday decoration she'd ever seen before. Floridian Christmas displays were given to garish plastic — with life-sized crèches set up on the burnt lawns of churches, inflatable Santas bobbing preposterously against the blue sky, and fake snow sprayed onto helpless palm trees. For Phoebe, a crèche like this really made her think of the historical version of Jesus' birth — which was the whole point, right? — and she liked the idea that it was simple and elegant but still beautiful.

As they stood there admiring it, Kate went to settle the baby Jesus softly into his cradle, but Gee gently stopped her, saying they wouldn't put him in until Christmas Eve, when Jesus had arrived for real. Although she didn't show it, the very idea raised goosebumps along Phoebe's arms. *Yes!* she thought. For this was just the kind of Christmas purity she was seeking! It wasn't about sales at Wal-Mart or plastic flamingoes; it was about keeping to the history of Christmas and the beautiful story that explained it all. She'd never heard of this particular tradition before, but she would certainly make a note of it in her file later.

Phoebe sighed with content and, while Kate tucked Jesus back into his cottony jewel box, and stowed it in the drawer of the side table until the twenty-fourth, Phoebe returned to the packing box she had selected. She'd been disappointed when she opened it, because it had turned out to contain Gee's collection of angels — and Phoebe thought angels were useless. To her, it seemed that the dopiest people believed in angels. Now granted, Phoebe didn't know much about religion or the Bible or whatever, but if there was life after death (which she desperately hoped there was, since she was terrified of dying), she sure hoped it wasn't full of halo-wearing harp players. That would be horrible!

Besides, there was a matter of taste. Phoebe felt that all the angel gear she'd ever seen was junky and dumb. There was a big angel-themed store in the mall near her house, and whenever she passed it, it was full of retirees — older women who'd chucked their pasts to move down to Nowhereville, Florida, and waste their pensions on junk to clutter up their condos. It was just ghastly.

Phoebe stewed about all of this while she unwrapped the angels from their white tissue and lined them up on the floor for consideration. Had Gee's collection not been so beautiful, Phoebe's evening would have truly been soured by having selected this box. But because she loved Gee, she worked diligently. Gee explained that some of the angels were antiques she had inherited, some she had bought from craftspeople on Gull or at craft shows on the mainland, and others were just gifts from people who knew of her Christmas collection. And actually, Phoebe noted, none were plastic.

When Phoebe had finished placing the angels around the room, singly and in groups, she returned to the empty box and gave a last rustle around the loose tissue at the bottom. But there was one more soft object in a corner. Unwrapping it, she caught her breath. It was one last angel. Although humble, it had been carefully made, with great skill. It had plain burlap robes, and soft, white linen wings on its back, sewn on with tiny, even stitches. The face was made of painted bisque, and had beautiful but simply painted features — bright blue eyes, rosy cheeks, red lips smiling gently — and dark brown hair (real, Phoebe guessed, successfully replacing her squeamishness with admiration for the craftsmanship) that was topped with a simple halo made of gold threads wound around and around into a thick, loose circle. For all of her negative feelings about angels, Phoebe had to admire the true beauty of this masterpiece. She could just imagine someone a hundred years ago making the body out of cloth in a quiet workshop somewhere in Maine, and taking great care to shape, fire, and paint the gorgeous and delicate face. Phoebe straightened its robes gently and asked, "Gee? Where did you *get* this one? It's beautiful."

Gee smiled and came over to sit on the upholstered bench next to Phoebe. Carefully, she took the angel from Phoebe's hands and lifted her glasses to her nose to give it a closer look. "Your grandfather gave it to me. It's funny you should ask about this one, because it started the whole collection. He bought it for me when we were engaged, from a boutique on Newbury Street in Boston." Gee smiled wryly and handed it back to Phoebe. "He said it looked like me."

Phoebe looked down at the angel and then back at Gee. She glanced at an old studio portrait of Gee in her wedding dress that sat on a skirted table by the fireplace. She was lovely, in a high-necked lace wedding dress, with long sleeves, her wavy dark hair caught back romantically in a low, loose bun, and a happy look on her unlined face. Gee looked like an angel herself in the photo.

"He was right," agreed Phoebe. "Where should I put it?"

"I usually put it over there, on the mantel," said Gee with a wave of her hand. "But you could put it anywhere you like."

Phoebe thought for a moment. In her file, one of the pictures had a sweet tree with an angel on top. It looked beautiful. "Can we save it for the top of the tree?" Phoebe asked.

Gee chuckled. "If you think it's worthy."

Phoebe looked down at the angel again. "Yes. I do," she said, and she stood and placed the angel on the mantel for the time being. Then she stretched and surveyed the room. Hillary had lined up a group of European-looking elves and Santas on the rug, and Gee was instructing her to bring them to the sideboard in the dining room. Neeve had just unpacked an old music box in the shape of a wintry, German-looking log cottage that played "Oh Tannenbaum" when you lifted the roof. She placed it on the coffee table. And then Sheila briefly popped in with boxes of candy canes in a grocery bag, and a few boxes of assorted chocolates that Gee liked to keep out in the living room for visitors.

After a quick bite-sized chocolate-covered caramel, Phoebe returned to her box to gather up the loose tissues and carry it all back up to the attic. The flaps on the cardboard box fluttered like wings as she hoisted it up on her shoulder. But suddenly, there was a sickening crash, and Phoebe wheeled around to see what had made the noise.

"Oh no!" she cried. It was the angel, Gee's first angel. When Phoebe had hoisted the box onto her shoulder, one of the flaps must've skimmed the mantel and knocked down the angel. Phoebe's heart was thudding in her throat and her face burned with shame. She put the box carefully aside and knelt to lift the angel from where it had fallen, facedown on the brick surround of the fireplace.

As soon as she picked it up, she could feel from the weight of it what she'd done. Its entire face was shattered. Hot tears sprang to Phoebe's eyes, and she looked up to see that Gee had crossed the room to stand by her. Everyone else was silent. Phoebe looked around and saw the anguish on Kate's face, Hillary biting her lip, and Neeve, her little mouth in an *O* and both hands covering it in shock.

Gee knelt down next to Phoebe and put her hand on Phoebe's back.

"I'm so sorry, Gee. I am *so* sorry," Phoebe repeated over and over like a mantra. It seemed that if she said it enough, it would undo the damage she'd caused.

"It's alright, sweetheart. It was an accident. It's not your fault." Gee gingerly took the angel from Phoebe's hands and examined its face. It was clearly broken beyond any possibility of repair. Gee looked up at Phoebe and saw the tears streaming down her face and instantly wrapped her in a hug. Phoebe sat erect, her arms at her sides, while Gee hugged her. Phoebe was not really into hugs, even when she was sad. But Gee knew that, and pulled away so as not to make Phoebe uncomfortable for any longer than was necessary.

"Oh, my dear, it's just an object. It's just like anything — its time had come. It had to go," Gee laughed gently to show she was joking. "Don't be sad. You didn't mean to break it. And I will certainly survive without it. I could survive without any object, but I could never survive without my wonderful grandchildren, and that's what's important."

Phoebe was still speechless with shame and sadness. She took a ragged breath and drew her sleeve across her face to mop up the tears. Gee produced a fresh holly-sprigged handkerchief from her pocket and handed it to Phoebe.

"Blow," she instructed.

Meanwhile, the other girls had come to Phoebe's side.

Neeve and Hillary murmured comforting things, and then Kate came to give Phoebe a big hug, which Phoebe received stiffly.

"Don't worry, Bee," said Kate. "We can still find something really great for the top of the tree."

And Phoebe had to laugh. "Kate! I'm not crying because we don't have something for the top of the tree! I'm crying because I broke Gee's present from Pops. Her most treasured decoration that looked just like her!"

Gee sat back on her heels. "Oh pshaw!" she said with a smile. "I never did see the resemblance. Now you just stop all this nonsense. I'll survive without her. You know, when you live for sixty-five years, you break quite a lot of lovely things, and honestly, girls, after a while, you just know not to get to attached to any object. I mean it." She reached over to pat Phoebe on the head, and then she stood up.

"I'm going to go get the broom and dustpan to sweep up the crumbs. If you hand me the rest of it I'll throw it away when I'm in there." Gee stretched out her hand to receive what was left of the angel: her body, and the back part of her head, which gruesomely had the hair and the halo still attached to it.

"Sorry," mumbled Phoebe uselessly.

▲

Later, Phoebe lay in her bed, her little portable reading light shining onto her lap, where *Dr. Zhivago* lay unopened.

"I still can't believe I did it," Phoebe said to Hillary, who was trying to go to sleep in the next bed.

"Hrumph," grunted Hillary. They'd been over this a few times now since it had happened. First Phoebe had had to recreate the scene, trying to figure out how it had happened. Then she'd wanted to discuss going online to try to research the maker, so she could try to buy a replacement for Gee. But they'd quickly established (after digging in the trash) that there were no maker's marks of any kind on what was left of the figure, so such a process would be near impossible. Finally, she'd wanted to review Gee's reaction over and over again, trying to gauge just how upset Gee really was. And no amount of consolation from the cousins would convince Phoebe that they all thought Gee was okay with it. She was sure Gee was crying into her pillow down the hall, and that it was all her, Phoebe's, fault.

And now Phoebe had privately decided that the angel had broken to teach her a lesson. She shouldn't have been thinking such bad thoughts about angels while she was unpacking them, and the breakage had been her punishment. And the extra punishment had been that she had not had the heart to share her Proper Christmas file with the cousins when they'd all come up to their rooms. It hadn't seemed appropriate, and she'd been too despondent to even begin.

She sighed and opened to the page she'd left off with in *Dr. Z*, but she didn't read it immediately. Instead, she thought about what an incredibly long day it had been: her journey up from Florida, getting the tree, the sleepover announcement. . . . Ugh. The sleepover. She had to figure out how they could avoid inviting Sloan, who would ruin it for sure. But not now. Now, she had to read or she'd never be able to go to sleep.

CHAPTER FIVE

Taffy

$\mathcal{A}$s usual, Hillary woke Phoebe up way too early the next morning.

"Bee! It's snowing!" she cried from the window, where she was peering out through the lifted shade.

Phoebe sat up. "What?" she asked groggily. She was determinedly not a morning person — it wasn't that she needed so much sleep, just that she always stayed up too late reading. Last night it had been nearly one in the morning when she'd turned out her light. She'd finished *Dr. Zhivago* and, as was her habit, had had to start a new book, so she'd have something new to look forward to. She could never just finish a book and put it down and go to sleep; she had to be engaged in the next one first. "Chain reading" her mother called it, as Phoebe moved from the end of one book to the beginning of the next.

"Snow!" repeated Hillary excitedly.

Phoebe flopped back onto her pillows. "I would think that you, of all people, would have seen enough snow to last a lifetime," she said in her fake-grouchy morning voice. (Hillary lived in Denver and spent all winter skiing and snowboarding after school and on weekends.) But inside, Phoebe was elated. Here it was, her first full day on the island, and it had snowed! Now they'd have a white Christmas for sure! She was paralyzed with excitement, not sure whether to run to the window first, change into the unfamiliar winter clothes she'd brought, or roll over and go back to sleep, which was what her body wanted her to do. So instead of doing any of those things she just lay there.

"Come on! Get up, lazybones! Let's go outside and play."

Suddenly, Kate and Neeve burst into the room.

"It's snowing! It's snowing!" Neeve sing-songed, as she danced around the room, pointing her fingers up in the air. Her green batik nightgown swirled and ballooned around her ankles.

Kate hugged herself and smiled. "Maybe we could go make maple syrup taffy after breakfast!"

Phoebe sat up now, wide awake.

"I have been dying to do that for my whole life," she announced somberly.

"Shut up, Bee!" said Kate, sure that Phoebe was teasing her.

"No! I'm serious! Ever since I read it in *Little House in the Big Woods* when I was six or something. I've always wanted to do it!"

"Well then let's get going!" said Kate with a cheerful grin, relieved that she wasn't the butt of a joke.

"Can we make a snowman?" Phoebe asked, throwing back her covers.

Hillary snapped up the shade and studied the snow for a minute. "It's hard to say. It might be good packing snow and it might not; depends on the flake size, and how dry it is."

Phoebe had no snow experience, so what Hillary was saying was like Greek to her. Still, Phoebe sighed happily and slid out of bed, coming to join Hillary at the window.

"Snowball fight?" she asked hopefully, surveying the transformed landscape. The lawn was entirely white, and the trees had a thin coating on their branches. Phoebe folded her arms across her chest; a chill wind was slipping in through the cracks around the old window panes.

"Maybe. We'll just have to see."

Kate raised her eyebrows. Usually she and Phoebe were the indoors cousins, while Neeve and Hillary were the outdoors cousins. Kate was clearly feeling abandoned by Phoebe in Phoebe's sudden new snow fascination.

"Sledding?" prodded Phoebe, ignoring the expression on Kate's face. She had an agenda and she wasn't going to let Kate hold her back now. Especially when it came to snow!

Hillary bent her knees and stared intently out the window. "If it keeps snowing this hard for another hour, there should be enough snow to do some sledding, for sure."

Phoebe leaned up against the windowsill.

"Where would we go?" she asked.

"We could call Lark . . . ," offered Hillary.

But with Lark might come Sloan. Blast! thought Phoebe.

"Or Talbot! He'd know for sure!" interjected Neeve brightly.

"Yes," agreed Phoebe animatedly. "Will you call him?" she asked.

"Yes, but first, let's all get dressed and go downstairs!" ordered Neeve, and she herself flounced out of the room to shed her pj's.

Phoebe turned to search out the clothes she'd unpacked the night before, and Kate reluctantly trailed Neeve back to their room to get dressed.

Soon, they were all dressed and in the kitchen, ready for the taffy-making to begin. Phoebe was dressed somewhat stiffly in an unfamiliar collection of new and borrowed clothes: flannel-lined jeans she'd borrowed from a friend back home, a blue turtleneck her mom had ordered for her from L.L. Bean just for this trip, and a thick, heathery green wool sweater she'd inherited from Daphne, who'd picked it up years ago on a ski trip with a friend's family. It had suede elbow patches and was long on her. She was warm but somewhat laden down with the weight of everything. But despite the slight discomfort, she was thrilled to have reason to wear the warm clothes, what with the deepening snow outside and the strong wind rattling the panes of Gee's waterfront windows. Her happiness was shadowed slightly by the memory of the previous evening's broken angel coupled with anxiety about the sleepover, but other than that Phoebe was very content.

"And to think I just said last night that our snow doesn't usually stick! Ha!" Gee stomped her feet on the mat as she came in through the back door and everyone did a double take when they saw her. She had just been for her daily swim in the frigid waters of the sound, and had a towel slung around her neck. But unlike her summer swimming attire, Gee now had on a head-to-toe winter "dry suit" (a dry suit keeps you completely dry in the water, she explained, while a wetsuit actually allows water to circulate next to your skin) with a hood, boots, and mittens to keep her warm and snug in the freezing water.

The girls laughed in surprise, and Gee modeled the suit for them, and then dashed upstairs to shower and change. Phoebe marveled at Gee's youthfulness and energy, and her dedication to her daily ritual of an early swim and then church. But Gee always said it was the swimming and church that kept her young. The swimming for her body, and mass for stress relief and a sort of meditation that cleared her mind. It obviously worked, although Phoebe couldn't really relate to all that church.

The snow had knocked Phoebe's school vacation morning routine all out of whack. Usually she'd eat in her pj's, do the crossword puzzle in its entirety, then get dressed and move on with her day. But today, she was dying to get outside and feel the snow all around her, so she'd dressed early, skipped the crossword, and volunteered to be the collector for the taffy project. She felt out of sorts, but in a good way — like she'd been cut loose, untethered.

She quickly put on her hat, scarf, mittens, coat, and boots, then she turned stiffly and said in a voice muffled by her scarf, "Do you think I'm dressed warmly enough?"

Everyone laughed at her precautions.

"You are so cute, you little beach bunny!" said Kate.

"You're only going outside the back door," added Hillary, grinning.

But Phoebe didn't care that they were laughing at her. She opened the back door and braced herself against the chill wind as she stepped off the back porch and pulled the door closed behind her. Her feet squeaked on the new snow, and everything was quiet, which surprised her. She couldn't remember ever being in falling snow. Maybe once in Sweden, when she was little, and one other time on a trip to visit Kate, but that was it. She realized now that she had kind of expected snow to make a noise when it fell, like rain, but instead, it was the opposite — it silenced things.

She looked around for a nice clean patch of snow, and finding one, squatted to scoop up spoonfuls into the aluminum mixing bowl Sheila had given her. Looking over her shoulder to make sure no one was spying on her, she took a big mouthful of snow and ate it. It packed against the roof of her mouth like Styrofoam, but quickly melted, leaving her teeth cold and her throat stinging. It didn't have much taste, but the sensation was fascinating, so she did it a few more times.

Then she crab-walked across the grass to collect more snow because it wasn't quite deep enough to get it all in one spot. She quickly filled the bowl, and after smiling at the funny tracks she'd made in the snow, she stood up and rushed back into the house, not wanting it all to melt before they had a chance to do the taffy thing.

Back inside, she ditched her boots and other gear, and scurried across the floor in her damp socks to dole out the snow. With fluffy white flakes melting on her hair, she placed a big scoop of snow on a plate for each cousin. This the girls flattened out, per her instructions (memorized from the photocopied scene that was in her file upstairs) and then they took turns pouring a little pan of maple syrup over the snow in swirly designs. The syrup hardened quickly and they picked it up to savor the chewy sweet gobs of confection. Phoebe sighed blissfully. It was as good as she'd always hoped it would be.

"Heavenly," she declared, and the others laughed again at her euphoria.

Gee returned shortly, gulping some coffee and stealing a spoonful of Phoebe's taffy. Dressed in charcoal gray wool pants, low black snow boots, and a shawl-necked gray cashmere cardigan belted over her white blouse, she was off to church. Phoebe watched her closely for any sign of anger or regret about the angel, but there was none. Phoebe's dad had always said that his mother got over things quicker than anyone he knew. One of her mottoes was "Next case." It meant "Move on" and "Don't dwell on something." And now Phoebe could see what he was talking about. It didn't make her feel better about what she'd done, but at least she knew Gee wasn't mad at her. In fact, Gee planted a kiss specially on Phoebe's head before she left for church.

On her way out Gee called over her shoulder that there were some old-fashioned sleds in the garage, and this reminded Phoebe of her Proper Christmas file.

"Nobody move!" said Phoebe. "I'm going to get something to show you."

"Can I just call Talbot about sledding?" asked Neeve, already out of her seat.

Phoebe squinted at her. "Oh, okay, but nobody else!" And she darted up the stairs.

Moments later, Phoebe was back with the green file folder in her hands. Neeve had successfully arranged not only for them to meet Talbot at the sledding hill, but also for Lark's dad to come pick them up at ten and give them a ride to the hill with Lark. Phoebe was pleased with Neeve's efficiency and very excited about the sledding, and much relieved to hear that it would only be Lark, and no one else.

"Now," she began, sliding in to the banquette. Hillary was playing with the remains of her maple syrup taffy, and Kate was looking at a decorating magazine. Neeve was flipping through the pages of the *Boston Globe,* and no one seemed interested in the file Phoebe had placed neatly on the table in front of her.

"Ahem," she began again, minutely aligning the corners of the folder to be perfectly square to the corner of the table.

The others looked up.

"Now that I have your attention," Phoebe said. "I'd like to discuss our holiday plans."

Neeve giggled. "Why? Are you thinking of celebrating differently this year?"

Hillary smiled, and Kate looked nervous, as she always did when new plans were afoot.

Phoebe was serious, though. "Yes. I am," she said. She laid her palms flat on the file.

"Okay-y-y . . . ," said Neeve. "How?"

"As you know, I live in Florida. . . ."

"Yeah, we'd heard that," laughed Hillary, rolling her eyes at Neeve as if to say *"What's come over Phoebe?"*

Phoebe frowned at them, then looked down at her file and continued. "And I have never had, a, um, a proper Christmas, if you follow me. . . ." She cleared her throat, and looked up at them again. The three cousins were staring at her in confusion, their brows furrowed as if they were struggling to understand her.

"What do you mean?" said Kate finally. "Don't you celebrate Christmas?"

Phoebe sighed in exasperation, and blurted, "Of course I

do, you nitwit! I've just never had a snowy, old-fashioned, New England Christmas before." The seriousness of the moment was somewhat shattered by Phoebe's outburst, but at least now she'd said it. She'd practiced explaining it to them in her mind so many times and now all of the rehearsed phrases escaped her, but she took a deep breath and tried to rephrase what she'd said.

"Okay. I want us all to have a really traditional Christmas this year. This is my one chance to do it, for the foreseeable future anyway, and it's something I've always wanted. I propose a Christmas free of tacky commercialism and plastic doohickeys, a Christmas instead full of meaning and beauty and, to say it again, tradition. I think this can all be accomplished in a multitude of ways, both indoors and out, and what follows is my proposal." And now, at last, Phoebe opened the cover of her folder to begin the presentation.

"I think I only understood about half of the words in your speech, but I'm catching your drift," said Neeve with a mischievous smile.

Phoebe huffed at Neeve and continued.

"For starters, I want to do all kinds of indoors stuff to prepare for Christmas: crafts and baking and everything." She looked at Kate as she said this. Kate loved crafts and cooking, and would be sure to enjoy baking old-fashioned sugar and gingerbread cookies, and crafting custom Christmas stockings from red felt and glitter. Now Phoebe licked her finger and flicked through about ten sheets of paper (photocopies and pages neatly razored from magazines), gathered them into a small pile, shook them on edge to square them up, and then slid them across the table to Kate. Kate eagerly pulled them across the white quilted tablecloth and tuned Phoebe out while she began browsing through them.

Neeve and Hillary were still looking at Phoebe in a disbelief, but she ignored their expressions and bent down to her file again.

Since Hillary was athletic and outdoorsy, she would be charged with anything of that ilk. "Hillary, I'd like to make a snowman, have a snowball fight, forage in the woods for Christmas greenery, ice skate on a pond if possible, and go for a horse-drawn sleigh ride." She selected a group of pages for Hillary and slid them to her. Hillary looked at the pages and then looked back at Phoebe, her face a mask of disbelief. Then she paused to scan the pages Phoebe had handed her.

It seems to be going well so far, Phoebe told herself. *It was a good idea to parcel out the assignments like this, playing to people's areas of expertise.*

"Now, Neeve," said Phoebe, looking Neeve squarely in the eye (for she'd gained confidence at this point). "You are the social coordinator. You've already coordinated a sledding outing, but I'd also like to go caroling, which I believe you indicated you had already begun to arrange, and . . ." Here, Phoebe paused for dramatic effect. When she had gotten everyone's attention she said, "I'd like to have a big Christmas party."

Neeve squealed and clapped her hands. "Yes! Totally! Brilliant! Genius!"

Phoebe beamed with pleasure. "Thank you," she said, modestly ducking her head.

Kate's eyes were shining. "We could have delicious hors d'oeuvres . . . ," she began.

"Just so long as we have baked Brie," said Phoebe. She'd had it at a party at Kate's friend's house once and still recalled it fondly whenever hors d'oeuvres were mentioned.

"Sure," agreed Kate with a smile. "With chutney, and French bread to spread it on. Just like Gretchen's mom makes it."

"And warm curried chicken salad," added Neeve. "In little pastry cups with shredded coconut on top. We have those when we're in Dublin for Christmas sometimes."

Hillary chimed in. "My mom always makes these mini-meatloaf thingies, with ketchup, on soft bread."

"Sounds yummy," said Kate. "I should be taking notes."

"Don't worry. We'll remind you," said Phoebe. "In addition, I have a large assortment of recipes here for things like an old-fashioned *bouche de noel,* which is a Christmas cake shaped like a log, and I thought we could make or even buy a really beautiful gingerbread house as a centerpiece for the party. . . ."

Kate laughed excitedly. "Yes, so we'll do a big buffet and then have the cake and also pass Christmas cookies for dessert. We can make the cookies ourselves and decorate them. . . ."

"I have the recipe for Royal Icing right here," said Phoebe, eagerly flipping pages.

"Don't worry, I know it by heart," said Kate with a dismissive wave of her hand.

With all the good feelings in the air, Phoebe decided the moment was right to go for the clincher. "And no store-bought presents. Only homemade gifts. Gifts from the heart," she added piously.

The others turned and looked at her. "Wait, *what*?" said Hillary.

"For Christmas this year, I propose we make gifts for each other and Gee, Sheila, whomever. In *Little House in the Big Woods*, for example, Ma Ingalls knit red mittens for the girls, and in *Anne of Green Gables*. . . ."

"Hang on!" interrupted Neeve. "I don't knit, sister, and if you think I'm slaving over some crummy project that will turn out gross when I could instead be buying you something that is just perfect in a store instead, you are crazy. No way!"

Hillary was nodding in agreement. "I'm with Neeve. I am not a gift-maker. I'll just buy you something cool downtown. You'll love it. You'll see."

But Phoebe was shaking her head. "No. That's what I'm saying. I don't want anything store-bought. If this is going to be a traditional Christmas, I only want things that are hand-made. No commercialism. I hate all that 'Hot Toy of the Year' hype; it's just wrong."

"I think it's a neat idea," offered Kate. Phoebe smiled at her in gratitude.

"Whatever, Laura Ingalls," said Neeve. "Dictating what people give you isn't really in the Christmas spirit anyway. Maybe I'll just give you *nothing*!"

"That would be preferable to some mass-marketed hunk of junk." Phoebe closed her file and folded her hands on top of it. She looked at Neeve serenely.

"Ugh!" Neeve huffed in annoyance. "The nerve of you, you . . . you . . . selfish . . ."

Kate hated fighting. "Listen, everyone," she said anxiously. "Let's not worry about the present thing right now. Christmas really isn't about presents anyway, or it shouldn't be, right, Phoebe?" Here, Phoebe nodded, of course. "Let's all just focus on the fun activities Phoebe mentioned, and we'll just have a great time and not worry about gifts for a little while, okay?"

Neeve eyed Phoebe until Phoebe nodded her head, then Neeve reluctantly nodded hers, too.

CHAPTER SIX

Snow!

$\mathscr{T}$he time had passed quickly while they were discussing the Proper Christmas and the sleepover, and now they had to hurry to get ready for Lark Kendo and her dad.

Gee had laid out some extra snow clothes on the landing at the top of the stairs, and Phoebe was pleased to discover a pair of ski pants that were big enough for her to borrow, and combined with the winter jacket she'd borrowed from her friend Jane back home, she would be warm and dry. She dressed quickly and gratefully accepted Hillary's advice on how to tuck her gaiters into her boots, and later, her mittens up into her jacket, to keep the snow from going up her sleeves or the legs of her pants.

Hillary was suited up in seconds; she had to jump into her snow gear a couple of times a day in the winter when she was home, so she was very speedy. And Kate had a cute one-piece snowsuit that she just wiggled into and zipped. She said it kept her so warm and dry she could probably swim in the sound in it, just like Gee in her dry suit. Everyone laughed at the very idea of Kate going in the sound in the winter. It was hard enough to get her in in August!

Neeve had had the foresight to e-mail Hillary and ask her to bring along some old snow gear for her to borrow. The resulting pale blue shell and bib pants were three years old (because Neeve was so much tinier than Hillary) and embroidered with flowers; clearly selections from the little girl's department. But Neeve, with her usual fashion sense, added a tight black turtleneck sweater with thick ribbing, a groovy sheepskin sherpa hat from a trip she'd taken to Nepal, and the big, tie-dyed pashmina that she tied this time like a kimono sash around her waist to cinch the boxy jacket. Phoebe marveled at the transformation.

Once bundled, the girls trudged out to the garage to gather up the sleds. Phoebe loved the prickle of the cold snowflakes alighting on her face like falling stars, and she stopped to inspect the ones that perched on her jacket before they were blown away. They were intricately beautiful and clean-looking, and much more delicate than she had ever realized. She tipped her head back and held out her tongue, as she'd seen Neeve doing, and the tickle of the flakes as they landed on her tongue caused her to giggle lightheartedly. Before they reached the garage, Neeve laid down on the lawn and began sliding her arms and legs around in great arcs. Phoebe stared at Neeve's bizarre behavior for a moment before she realized what Neeve was doing.

"Snow angels!" cried Phoebe. And she flopped down next to Neeve to make her own, knowing a moment of fresh anguish as she was reminded yet again of Gee's broken angel. She swished her arms and legs up and down and looked at Neeve to check that she was doing it right. When she seemed finished she asked, "How do I get up without ruining it?" and Neeve showed her how to lever herself up and throw herself out of the imprint without doing too much damage.

Phoebe stood and admired her own handiwork, and Neeve's tiny angel, beside it. "Wow," she breathed. They really did look like angels. Even with her disdain for angels, she had to admit these were beautiful things to see carved out of the snow.

"Bee! Neeve! We found them!" Phoebe turned to see Hillary dump two scavenged sleds on the driveway outside the garage and then duck back in for a plastic toboggan. Phoebe and Neeve went to help, and they dragged it all to the edge of the driveway by the back door for when they got picked up.

Right then, Gee pulled up and asked that they pick a night for the sleepover. She needed to call the museum director because she'd promised to set a date before the weekend — it being Friday — and Monday seemed like the best choice. Everyone readily agreed, even Phoebe, but her stomach clutched. She still hadn't come up with an idea for how she could avoid having to invite Sloan.

Gee ducked into the house to call the director of the museum while they waited for the Kendos, and Neeve spoke up.

"So who are we having?" she asked mildly, looking around.

Phoebe sighed heavily. "I *really* don't want her to come. . . ." Everyone knew she meant Sloan. Sloan always changed the tone of things. She took over, or she created some drama, or she was just plain mean. "She would totally ruin it. You know how she is. . . ."

"I don't think she *has* to be invited," interrupted Hillary, her palms in the air.

"Not if it's going to ruin things for you, Bee." Kate looked at her sympathetically.

And now everyone looked at Neeve. "I guess this Christmas is going to be all about what Phoebe wants," said Neeve brattily.

"Neeve!" said Kate in dismay.

"Well, it's true. As long as we all know that going into it, it won't be so difficult."

Phoebe was stung by Neeve's comment, partially because she knew it was true, or seemed that way so far. She opened her mouth to say something — an apology, a defense — but Gee came out and they all turned to look at her expectantly.

"Sleeping bags. Warm pajamas. Pillows. Picnic dinner. Change of clothes. Toiletries. Teddy bears." She winked at the girls and they laughed. "It's all settled. It sounds fun! They have a new young employee at the museum, Jessica somebody or other, who will be your chaperone, and you're going to do an old-fashioned craft, and hear some Christmas stories, and sing some old carols. It should be terrific!"

"Great! Thanks, Gee," said Phoebe. She was so excited she

wouldn't let anything dim her feelings. At least not for the moment.

"Gee, one more thing . . . ," began Neeve, looking around at the others for support.

Phoebe was aghast. Neeve wouldn't dare draw Gee into this whole thing about it being "Phoebe's Christmas," would she?

The smiles on Kate and Hillary's faces faded as they wondered what Neeve was about to say.

"Could we have a, um, Christmas party, maybe, one night? Like for your friends and ours? Sort of a big traditional celebration?" She looked at Phoebe as she emphasized the word "traditional."

"Oh!" That wasn't what Phoebe had expected to hear coming out of Neeve's mouth. She held her breath, hoping Gee would say yes.

"Like an open house?" asked Gee. The girls all nodded. "I think that's a wonderful idea! Let's!"

Kate clapped and Phoebe beamed and Neeve gave Gee a big hug. "Thanks, Gee. You're the best grandma in the whole world!"

"I don't know about that . . . ," said Gee, laughing at Neeve's heavy praise.

Phoebe was so excited, she could hardly breathe. Why had Neeve done that? And why hadn't she said anything about Sloan?

Now Hillary squared her shoulders. "And we've decided that there will only be five of us at the sleepover. Just Lark and us, okay?" She looked at Neeve with a challenge in her eye, and Neeve shrugged ever so slightly. Phoebe watched the scene in astonishment. Could it really have been that easy?

"We don't have to have six people, do we, Gee?" added Kate.

Gee's head was tilted thoughtfully to the side. "Absolutely not. So no Sloan?" she asked mildly, her eyebrows raised as she looked from face to face.

Everyone shook her head no.

"I think that's a wise decision," said Gee. "Somehow, when Sloan gets involved, there are always hurt feelings or some kind of trouble."

Now that Phoebe had gotten her way, she felt a stab of guilt. It wasn't really in the Christmas spirit to exclude someone.

"So, back to the party . . . ," said Gee.

And then Phoebe had a brainstorm that made her feel instantly better. "I know! We could invite Sloan to the Christmas party! That way, there will be enough people so that I can kind of stay away from her, but you all can talk to her as much as you want."

Gee clapped her hands together. "I think that's a wonderful idea, Phoebe my dear. That way no one feels left out."

Phoebe looked at Neeve and Neeve seemed satisfied, which made it all seem okay.

The Kendos' dark blue SUV pulled in at the bottom of the driveway and began its ascent up the mild slope of Gee's driveway. Mr. Kendo honked the horn twice in greeting, and they all waved as he approached. Spying the cousins in the driveway, Lark had rolled down her window and was hanging out so far that Gee called, "Goodness, darling, don't fall out!"

Lark hopped out before her father had even pulled to a complete stop, and dashed as quickly as she could over to the girls. She had on pink snow pants and a puffy pink down jacket with the fake-fur trimmed hood pulled tightly over her head, and her hands were thrust deep into a pair of sturdy Gore-Tex gloves that reached well past her wrists. Her layers caused her to move slowly and stiffly, but she compensated by talking a mile a minute in her excitement.

"Hi, Gee! Hi, guys!" In order to talk, she had to lift her chin above the scarf wound around her neck. "I'm *so* happy you're back! I can't even *believe* you're here. This is the best Christmas present *ever*! I missed you all *so much*! I can't wait to hang *out*! Oh, it's just so great that you're *here*. I can't believe you're *really* here!" She hugged everyone, even Gee.

Phoebe received the hug awkwardly, as usual, but she laughed out loud at Lark's rush of words. She was as chatty as ever, and small and cute, like Neeve. And the way she called Gee *Gee* cracked Phoebe up; by the end of the summer, Lark had been practically living at The Sound, so she had become sort of an honorary cousin. "Hi, Lark!" Phoebe returned the greeting, as did the others, and they all scrambled to drag the sleds to the car and open the doors and clamber aboard.

Gee walked to Mr. Kendo's window to chat while the girls loaded in. When the last door slammed, she stepped away and waved. "I'll bring them back around one!" Mr. Kendo called.

Gee thanked him and then cupped her hands around her mouth and shouted "Goodbye, ducklings! Have fun!"

In the car, Lark took the front and the cousins piled into the middle row, but Lark turned around and leaned as far back as her seat belt would allow, so she might as well have been sitting with them. "I can't believe you're really here! I was so psyched when you e-mailed me to say you were coming! And then it seemed to take forever. How were your trips back? Hey, are you sad to be away from your families for Christmas? What are you doing about presents?"

"Lark, honey, let them get a word in edgewise," said Mr. Kendo, smiling at the girls in the rearview mirror and shaking his head. "Thank God you're back," he said to them. "We've had her all to ourselves all fall," he added, teasing. Lark pretended to swat him with the glove she'd removed, then she turned back to the cousins with an expectant look on her face.

"Well, our trips back here were uneventful," began Phoebe, looking to the others for agreement. "And I think we're all having a mock-Christmas with our parents when we get home, right?"

Neeve nodded. "Actually, my mom postponed Christmas for everyone. They decided to go to Fiji for ten days, and when I get back we're going to do the whole thing together."

"Nice!" said Lark.

Hillary nodded. "I did a mini-Christmas with my dad before I left, and my mom and I are going to go up to my other grandparents' when I get back and have a late Christmas there." Phoebe turned swiftly to look at Hillary for any signs of sadness; this was her parents' first Christmas apart since they'd officially decided to get divorced. But Hillary seemed to be taking it in stride.

"My family is going ahead with it and then I'm going to have my own private Christmas when I get back," said Kate. "Of course we did all the usual stuff before I left: set up the decorations, designed the color palette and scheme for the tree décor, which my mom and Julie were going to try to follow through without me. Oh dear, I hope Julie didn't break anything! And we made tons of cookies, plus the sweets and stuff that we give out as gifts to everyone, with the handmade labels — we did all that before I left."

Phoebe was impressed. Although all of this was totally in character, she hadn't realized that Kate did so much Christmassy stuff every year. She felt a twinge of jealousy; her family didn't do any of that kind of old-fashioned stuff.

Lark laughed. "And what are the big plans for your vacation here? You guys must have something cooked up."

"Actually . . . ," began Neeve, looking at the others for their permission.

"Yes!" said Phoebe. "Tell."

Lark's eyes lit up and she clapped her one gloved hand against her other bare hand, making a dull thudding noise as the girls told her about the plans for the sleepover and the Christmas party.

Mr. Kendo turned off the causeway and left onto Huckleberry

Lane. The trees arcing over the road were bare and black against the white sky, but an inch-thick layer of snow lay heavily on each branch, like frosting. They cruised slowly beneath the canopy of trees, and then the trees ended and a beautiful vista opened out to the farms on either side of the road. The summer corn had been cut down, and the fields were low and bare and starkly beautiful in their plainness. The falling snow made it hard to see all the way across the fields, and the wind blew in little fits and starts, lifting small tornadoes of snow from the ground, that would pirouette and then fall away.

"So where is this hill?" asked Phoebe.

"Just before the parking lot at Macaroni, we go left, and it's out on the bluffs. It's kind of a dirt road, and we have to walk the last little bit, but it's good when you get there."

Mr. Kendo made the turn, and the Suburban bumped slowly along the rutted road. They came to a small clearing, and four or five other vehicles were parked there, but it was by no means a crowd. They settled on a pickup time with Mr. Kendo, and with a wave of his gloved hand out the window, he was gone.

Standing in the parking lot, with the snow swirling lightly around them, the five girls looked at each other.

"Everyone ready?" said Hillary eagerly, stomping her boots.

"Ready as I'll ever be," Kate whimpered.

Chapter Seven

Sledding

𝒯he five girls proceeded through the narrow dune passage single file. As they walked, the muffled shrieks and shouts from the hillside were carried toward them on the light wind, and, looking forward to the possibility of seeing Talbot and some of their other summer acquaintances, not to mention sliding down the hill, Neeve and Hillary quickened their pace. Phoebe's fear of physical risk was growing as they drew closer, and Kate was in a dead panic.

The last bit of the walk was a straight climb uphill, and it was difficult going, but Lark coaxed Kate and Phoebe along, insisting it would be worth it, and when they reached the top, they saw that she was right. The view was impressive: In one direction, they could see the ocean over the grassy dunes, and in the other, they could see almost all the way back over the farm they'd just driven past. Phoebe was instantly transported to the snowy steppes of Dr. Zhivago's Russia, or the grassy plains of the Ingalls family homestead.

Even Phoebe could tell that this was the perfect place to sled. The hill they stood on was tall enough, but better than that, it ran down to a very low dip, like a valley, so the slope for sledding was nearly twice as long as it appeared from the other side of the hill. The dip rose gradually on the far side, so a speeding sled could simply coast toward the fields beyond, putting the brakes on naturally and offering no obstacles to crash into at the end of the run. The snow was about three or four inches deep now — not so deep that it was difficult to walk in, but deep enough to get a good ride. And the downfall seemed to be tapering off a bit, so the visibility was better than when they'd left Gee's.

There were about twenty people out on the hill — some grown-ups with a few little kids, and a handful of kids their age, more or less. The girls stood, looking carefully at the other kids, to see if they could recognize anyone, but everyone was so bundled up it was nearly impossible. They were used to seeing people on Gull in their bathing suits.

"Come on, let's hit it!" said Hillary with a whoop. She flopped down on her stomach on the sled she'd been carrying, and pushed herself forward with her arms, like she was paddling a surfboard. She quickly sped down the hill and zoomed up the far side, laughing and kicking her legs when she stopped.

"I feel sick," said Kate.

"Come on, Katie. I'll do it with you," offered Neeve, businesslike. "Don't you sled at home?"

"Sometimes, but . . . the hill's a little smaller. It's like a bunny hill."

Neeve pulled the saucer over and sat down with her little legs dangling over the sides. She patted the spot right in front of her. "Come on now, no time to waste!"

Reluctantly, Kate trudged over to Neeve and sat down heavily on the saucer. She'd barely arranged herself or had a moment to grasp the sides before Neeve had launched them, and despite her own nervousness, Phoebe laughed at Kate's shrieks as they spun and twisted down the side of the hill, landing in an unglamorous heap at the far side of the dip. They lay there, apparently laughing, and Phoebe was happy to see Kate had had a good first run.

Lark had an inflatable inner tube. "Want to come with me?" she asked Phoebe.

"Uh. . . ." Phoebe didn't like for someone else to be in control, but she could hardly insist on steering them when Lark was clearly the one with experience.

Lark peered closely at Phoebe. "Are you scared?" she asked. "You don't seem like you're ever scared of anything."

"Ha!" laughed Phoebe humorlessly, thinking of the many times she'd been scared just on Gull alone. But actually, it wasn't so much that the sledding scared her, as that she didn't want to end up looking like a big clumsy oaf. "Thanks, but you should go ahead. I've still got this other sled here." Phoebe looked down at the old wooden thing with its red metal runners. It was so old it looked like it had once belonged to the Bobbsey Twins or some 1950s family.

"Have you sledded before?" asked Lark.

"Barely. And not recently," admitted Phoebe.

"Tell you what," said Lark. "You take my sled — it's really easy. You just get on, hold on to the side handles, and I'll give you a push. This old sled of yours takes a little steering and stuff, and I know how to use it. Go on," she gestured generously. "I'll help you."

Cautiously, Phoebe lowered herself onto the tube. She folded her long legs like a pretzel, and, gasping as the sled began to move a little bit, she quickly grasped the handles. But Lark had grabbed the sled while Phoebe steadied herself. *It's kind of like getting into that tiny, tippy sailboat of Gee's,* she thought. Finally settled, Phoebe took a deep breath and nodded. Now Lark placed her hands on the back side of the tube and began to run a bit behind Phoebe. As the sled began to take off, she started to spin.

She tried to let go of her self-consciousness and just "be" in the moment, but it was hard for her. However, the sledding was really fun. As she entered her second rotation, she looked up at the top of the hill and saw someone arriving with a high-tech inflatable boat as a sled. The person had on beige snow pants with a matching jacket, a yellow hat over long dark hair, and a white scarf blowing out behind her like wings. *That person looks like Gee's angel!* Phoebe thought with a jolt. And then her tube spun 180 degrees, causing her to lose sight of the person. It was right then that she saw she was about to crash into a group of toddlers and she had to abandon ship, diving off the sled and landing hard on her side in a graceless flop, arms and legs sprawling.

And then she realized the person at the top of the hill — the angel look-alike — was Sloan.

"Ahhh!" Phoebe moaned in frustration as she sat up, wiping the snow where it had packed into her ear, and trying to dust it out of the collar of her jacket.

Lark ground to a stop beside her on the old-fashioned sled. Jumping up, she rushed to Phoebe's side.

"Oh my gosh! Are you okay? That was major!"

Phoebe looked up at the top of the hill and saw Sloan standing there. It was definitely her. Phoebe could tell now by the way she carried herself. She seemed to be waiting for Phoebe and Lark to clear out of the way so she could hit the slope, and her posture radiated that good old Sloan impatience: hand on hip, foot tapping, head held haughtily in the air.

I can't believe I thought she looked like Gee's angel, Phoebe thought, both mad at herself and mortified. "I'm fine. Thanks," she said to Lark in an unconvincing moan.

She rolled onto her hands and knees and slowly stood. Her hat had been yanked off by her fall and the sled had continued sliding beyond her, so she gingerly crunched through the snow to grab them. Her side ached, and while she was sure nothing was broken or twisted, she knew she'd have a really sore hip for the next few days. But even worse, her confidence was bruised and she was acutely embarrassed for having made such a spectacle of herself. This was definitely not what she'd had in mind for sledding.

Naturally the cousins came rushing over, and Phoebe fought off tears and humiliation, reassuring them that she was fine while still keeping one suspicious eye on Sloan. Luckily, they were quickly diverted.

"Look, guys, I see Talbot up there now!" said Neeve, always on the lookout for social opportunities. And it was. He was in black and silver snowboarding clothes, and looked as handsome as ever, even with the preposterously high-tech goggles perched up on his forehead. (Because he worked part-time at Booker's, the island's sporting goods store, he had all the latest gear.) He was waving vigorously, and Neeve and the others waved back. But Phoebe didn't wave because she was busy stealing a glance at Sloan, who, she figured, had just realized that it was the Callahans on their way up. Phoebe was already bracing herself for Sloan's opening remarks, which were sure to be catty and cutting and all about what a spazz Phoebe was.

Though they were now well to the side of the slope, and Sloan could have launched herself easily with no potential for interference, she stayed where she was, watching their climb. Phoebe wished herself elsewhere — back at Gee's, reading a book or doing the crossword puzzle in the cozy kitchen. But she wasn't. And now she was at the top of the hill and Sloan was standing not twenty feet away.

"Well, well, well, if it isn't the Callahan cousins, coming to partake of the winter tourist season here on Gull." Sloan was always calling them tourists, which rankled the Callahan girls. Though they weren't islanders, they were hardly day-trippers when they came to Gull, buying T-shirts or bumper stickers.

"Hey, Sloan!" said Kate warmly. Phoebe shot her a glance, but Kate didn't notice.

"Hiya, Sloanie!" said Neeve, giving Sloan a hug. *A hug!* thought Phoebe. *Traitor!*

Hillary and Lark greeted her and then Phoebe had to, too.

"Hello, Sloan," said Phoebe coldly.

"Hello, yourself. That was quite the yard sale you had down there."

"What?" Phoebe was confused, but Hillary smiled and turned to her.

"In skiing, when you wipe out and your skis and poles go fly-ing all over the slope, people call it a yard sale, because your gear is all spread around like you've laid it out for sale."

Phoebe looked at Sloan, who smirked. "Yeah. I guess that's what it was."

"Oh no, Phoebe. You sacrificed yourself. I was watching the whole thing. You would've totally whaled those toddlers if you hadn't abandoned ship. It was very brave of you." Kate was earnest in her praise, but despite the compliment, Phoebe didn't like the image of herself "whaling" anyone.

Phoebe harrumphed. "Anyway, it's over. And I think I'm over, too. I'm just going to watch for the rest of the time."

"Chicken?" said Sloan, with a challenging glint in her eye.

"Hardly," replied Phoebe.

Neeve and Hillary clomped over to talk to Talbot, and seemed from a distance to be making arrangements to ride down with him on the huge inflatable air mattress he'd brought. Next to Phoebe, Kate was saying she thought she might give it another whirl, if Lark went with her on Lark's tube.

Phoebe felt awkward. She didn't relish the idea of standing at the top of the hill by herself for the next hour an a half, but she was in pain still and a little gun-shy. Not to mention embarrassed. She folded her arms protectively across her chest and looked around for somewhere to sit where she'd be out of the way and inconspicuous, but still able to watch her cousins. And then Sloan said, "Want to come with me?"

It was about the last thing Phoebe had expected out of Sloan, and the last thing she wanted to do. She looked at Sloan, trying to judge if Sloan was mocking her, but there didn't seem to be the usual challenge in Sloan's eye. Phoebe sighed. Her defenses were down and suddenly she didn't know what to do.

"Come on," said Sloan, not pleading but not overly challenging either. Much to her surprise, Phoebe found herself actually considering it. Sloan's inflated boat looked comfortable and fun. "Get in! It'll be fun," ordered Sloan.

Looking back, Phoebe knew she'd still been in some sort of shock after her wipeout. But she found herself following Sloan's order without even realizing it. The next thing she knew, they were flying — really flying at one point when they hit a bump and went sailing into the air for a few seconds — and the wind was rushing in her ears, snowflakes blinding her and her stomach lifting and dropping as if she were on a roller coaster. "Wheee!" she heard someone yelling, and with a shock, she realized it was herself. Here she'd relinquished total control to Sloan, of all people, and she was actually enjoying it!

The inflatable boat was so slick on the bottom that they coasted well up the other side of the dip and onto the flats of the field beyond, where they slid another few feet and then collapsed, laughing and straightening their hats.

"Awesome!" cried Sloan, turning back with her hand held aloft for a high five.

Phoebe high-fived her back and then turned to see how far they'd come. They were way past where anyone else had gone, and Phoebe felt proud, like they'd won an Olympic event or something.

"I knew we could beat those pipsqueaks!" shouted Sloan.

"Huh," agreed Phoebe, shaking her head in wonder. They collected the boat and pulled it along sideways behind them, the boat thumping and rising at each bump in the snow.

Phoebe couldn't believe she'd just gone sledding with Sloan. This was definitely *not* in her file.

"It's been pretty dull around here without you guys," said Sloan quietly.

"I'm sure," said Phoebe wryly. As if Sloan didn't have a full enough plate bossing around all the islanders who were alternately in her thrall or under her thumb.

"No, really," said Sloan, turning to look at Phoebe.

Phoebe looked back at her, suspicious at first, but then finding no reason to be, she wasn't. "Thanks, I guess." She shrugged. She wasn't going to say she'd missed Sloan or anything. That wasn't true. And she couldn't think of anything fast enough to say in reply, so she just let Sloan's comment hang out there.

"Doing anything fun for Christmas?" Phoebe asked, just to make conversation.

"Nah. Just the usual. Some family parties where I'll be the oldest person there, with a bunch of snot-nosed brat friends of my brother's running around."

Phoebe laughed. "Sounds fun."

"What about you?"

"Oh. . . ." But she caught herself. She'd been about to mention the sleepover, but of course she couldn't. She thought fast to cover up the gaffe. "Um . . . we're having people over for a Christmas party next week. We haven't even planned it yet, but . . . we're going to invite you." Phoebe looked away. Why was she doing this? She knew Sloan would have to be invited, but she'd figured Kate or someone would do the inviting. Phoebe had already planned to spend the whole party avoiding her.

She glanced back at Sloan in time to see a small smile light up her face. Sloan looked down at the ground. "That would be really nice. Thanks. I'll come."

Phoebe was surprised. This was a side of Sloan that Phoebe had never seen. Maybe this was what the others were always talking about. The iceberg of Phoebe's dislike for Sloan suddenly melted just a tiny bit. *Like enough to fill a thimble,* Phoebe thought.

They reached the top of the hill and were met by cheers from the others, and Talbot, too.

"Nice ride, mon'!" he called through cupped hands. Phoebe smiled as he came over to say hello.

"Yeah, with Phoebe in the back as the anchor, we were able to use her weight to really get us sailing downhill!" said Sloan merrily, by way of explanation.

Phoebe felt like she'd been punched in the stomach. She knew that warm fuzzy feeling had been too good to be true. Her smile of victory froze on her face and she mentally kicked herself for ever issuing the party invitation to Sloan.

CHAPTER EIGHT

The Tree

The snow tapered off at midmorning, and by one o'clock the sun had come out. The wind still huffed in big gusts, but it blew the clouds away, to the east, out over the ocean, and the sky turned squinty-bright and blue.

The sledding had ended up okay. Sloan left just a half an hour after she'd arrived, then Mr. Kendo picked them all up as promised, and returned the girls and Lark to The Sound for lunch.

The tree had been delivered while the girls were sledding, and the first thing Phoebe did when she got home was to run into the living room to look at it. Its size was amazing. It scraped the high ceiling, and was wide and thick and bushy and so fragrant that the entire living room and front hall reeked of pine, in the best way. Phoebe just stood and stared at it, her heart swollen with joy. It was the most beautiful tree she'd ever had for Christmas, and she was proud of herself for choosing it (for now, in her mind, it *was* she who had chosen it). She was endlessly grateful to Gee for buying it, and she couldn't wait to gobble down her soup and sandwich and race back to start implementing her vision for the tree. But first, she ducked upstairs to her room and flipped open the file, laying it out across her bed. Quickly and deftly, she turned to the exact page she was looking for.

"Ahh." She sighed quietly in satisfaction. The tree on the page was tall, thick, and dark, just like the one that was sitting right now in the living room downstairs. It had heaps of white fairy lights twinkling along the branches, and plain, folksy ornaments, all in shades of oatmeal, pale denim blue, and faded red. It looked like the kind of tree you'd have if you lived on a large, old-fashioned farm, and snuck out into the wintry woods, and did up a living tree with all-natural sorts of decorations you'd either found or made with things from around the farm. Holding the magazine sheet in her hands, Phoebe lifted her eyes to imagine coming upon that very tree in the woods, candles lit all around it, woodland creatures peeping out of their dens in wonder, and the aroma. Mmm.

"Bee!" Kate was calling her from downstairs.

"Coming!" she called back in reply. She considered bringing the entire file down with her, but stopped herself. She felt funny about Gee seeing it; like, worried that Gee might think her fascination with it was strange or that Phoebe was somehow taking advantage of her. Using her, or something, just to get the Christmas of her dreams. But she couldn't help it; it might be her only chance in life. Quickly, Phoebe replaced the page in her file, stashed the file in her bedside table drawer, and dashed down to join the others.

Everyone, including Lark and Gee, had settled in the living room. Phoebe nipped back to the kitchen and grabbed the boom box, then loaded up an old *Nutcracker* tape of Gee's to set the mood. And while the music swirled around the girls in joyful bursts, they set about unpacking and laying out the ornaments for inspection.

Phoebe wanted only white lights, to simulate old-fashioned candles, so Neeve and Hillary, with a ladder and Lark to help, began the process of stringing the lights. Phoebe also wanted only handmade ornaments to go on the tree, and since Gee had given the girls the green light to do whatever they wanted, everyone had more or less agreed that that would be okay. Hillary had laughed, but Neeve had rolled her eyes. Kate was being helpful, reviewing the selections with Phoebe, while Gee looked on, a smile of amusement playing at the corners of her mouth.

Gee had a nice range of items from crafts fairs she'd attended over the years (she loved the work of artisans), both locally and abroad: little wooly lambs with black noses, quilted hearts, hand-carved reindeer, pigment-dyed wooden beads strung on a line for draping over branches. There were mini woolen Christmas stockings, hand-knit in Ireland; corn husk stars from the Midwest; carved Dutch clogs filled with pretend miniature treats, and so on. There were also quite a lot of beautiful glass balls, which Kate really wanted to add on, but Phoebe argued against them, saying they clashed with the look of the handmade things.

"I mean, if we were doing a Victorian theme, maybe. . . ." She bit her lip, wishing she could have her Proper Christmas file in front of her. Without the file, Phoebe struggled to verbalize the details of the image she'd pored over so many times.

Kate relented about the balls, but it wasn't easy for her. She considered her own taste excellent, and Christmas was an area of expertise for her, but it was becoming clear that this was going to be Phoebe's Christmas, just as Neeve had predicted.

Phoebe and Kate heaped the handmade ornaments back into their boxes and dragged them over to the tree. Hillary and Neeve were finishing up their work with the lights and it was almost time to start hanging the ornaments.

There was one last box still unopened, and Kate toed it toward Phoebe to take a look inside. They probably had enough stuff, but just in case, it was worth one more look.

Phoebe knelt down, unfolded the cardboard flaps, and rustled around in the tissue within. Inside were piles of plastic ornaments — some with cartoon characters from the 1970s holding artificial wreaths, some from travel destinations (Mickey Mouse sitting on a train that said "Merry Christmas from the Magic Kingdom!"), and even a Barbie in a white-fur trimmed Santa suit, with shorts instead of pants. Phoebe shuddered and began closing the flaps. She hadn't noticed Neeve peering over her shoulder.

"Wait! Those are great!" protested Neeve. "What are you doing with them?"

Phoebe looked at Neeve. "You're kidding, right?" said Phoebe.

Neeve looked at her in surprise. "No. I think we should have them! They're hilarious! Retro!"

Kate joined them and peered into the box. "Wow. You could get a lot of money on eBay for some of this stuff," she said to Gee. Gee shrugged. She didn't even know what was in there.

"And look." Neeve gestured to the side of the box where someone had scrawled in red ink "Kids' Faves." Underneath that, in red crayon — obviously written by a child — it said "I like Mickey best."

Phoebe studied the notes for a moment then looked back at Neeve. "That writing is obviously really old. No one who ever liked them is even a kid anymore."

"Come on, Phoebe! And anyway, what about tradition? Maybe your dad is the one who wrote that."

Phoebe shuddered, thinking of the plastic flamingos on the lawn. "He probably did. Which makes me want this stuff even less."

Gee had been listening in silence, an amused look on her face. She truly didn't care what they picked, but she was enjoying the process and loved listening to the girls' opinions and ideas. However, now, her brow furrowed. "Phoebe! That's not a very nice thing to say about your father!" she said lightly, to show she wasn't mad, just concerned.

Phoebe stood up and flopped hopelessly into a club chair. "But Gee," she began, fervently. "His version of Christmas is so . . . so . . . gross! He likes all this tacky plastic stuff. He thinks it's 'witty' and 'a slice of Americana.' And he and my mom are *so* not into Christmas, they like to make fun of it. Like, they think it's funny to have fondue for Christmas supper, instead of a big Christmas feast, and they like to go bowling on Christmas Day after we open our presents, and they wear these ugly Christmas sweaters as a joke, and . . . and . . ." *Oh no, she wouldn't cry! She couldn't let herself!*

Gee stood up and crossed the room to perch on the arm of Phoebe's chair, a worried look on her face. She put her hand on Phoebe's shoulder comfortingly and said, "Phoebe, sweetheart! Don't get yourself so upset. Now, just calm down and take a deep breath. It's just a tree."

Phoebe glanced at Lark, embarrassed that Lark was witnessing her Christmas meltdown. Lark looked like she was trying to disappear; she didn't know where to look, so she finally busied herself putting away the extra tree lights. Phoebe saw Neeve and Hillary exchange amused shrugs, so she knew she hadn't made them too mad, but Kate had a worried look on her face to match Gee's. Only Kate could truly relate to the frustration of having a decorating vision botched by compromise.

Phoebe took a deep breath. The tears subsided. She never, *ever* cried. Crying was childish, manipulative, and tacky, and she avoided it at all costs. "Gee, it's just, I've always wanted a nice Christmas. An old-fashioned, true blue, honest to goodness Christmas, like I've always read about and seen in movies and magazines. And it seemed like this was my best chance."

"Oh, sweetheart!" Gee rubbed Phoebe's back briskly and affectionately and looked at her in sympathy. "I am so sorry! I had no idea! Of course we'll make this a special Christmas for you. It will be wonderful and joyful and merry and all those good things." Gee chuckled for a second. "Your father! I can just see him, intellectualizing Christmas, turning tradition on its ear. That's just like him. Sometimes he's too smart for his own good!"

Phoebe smiled a wobbly smile. "He's a real pain!"

"I've thought the same thing myself, many a time," said Gee, smiling sympathetically. "But I'm sure he's lots of fun at Christmas, too."

Phoebe looked down at her lap, a little ashamed. "*He* thinks he is."

"Doesn't he do fun things with you kids to celebrate?"

Phoebe nodded.

"Come on now," bossed Gee. "Fess up. What does he do?"

Phoebe glanced up, and saw that everyone was watching her. She mumbled an answer, but no one could hear her.

"Say it again, sweetheart. We can't hear you."

"Christmas crab races," said Phoebe loudly and flatly.

Everyone laughed. "What the heck is *that*?" demanded Neeve, sputtering.

Phoebe didn't think it was that funny. She explained in an unamused tone, "We go down to the public beach, everyone finds a crab, you have to give it a Christmassy name, like Nick or Rudolph, and then we race them down the beach. My dad does the commentary, like it's a horse race. Now all of our friends come because they think it's so funny, and each year it gets a little bigger and a little more serious. He has a portable microphone and everything, now." Everyone else laughed again, but she twiddled her thumbs in her lap and didn't look up.

"That's wonderful!" said Gee merrily. "How creative!"

"It's not exactly Christmassy," said Phoebe, annoyed.

"What else do you do?" asked Lark, on the edge of her seat on the couch.

Phoebe sighed heavily. She was really not interested in revealing all of this to everyone, but it seemed like they weren't going to let her get away with just that. "Um, carol karaoke," she said quietly. But everyone heard.

Hillary clapped her hands. "Awesome! How do you do that?"

Phoebe looked up at her. "My dad has all these cheesy karaoke tapes of carols like 'Grandma Got Run Over by a Reindeer' that he plays on the karaoke machine, and everyone takes turns singing. Usually we have people over for that, friends of theirs from the hospital and their kids. I don't sing. I just watch a little or I sit in my room and read. Melody and Daphne love it." *Those traitors,* she added in her mind.

"Hilarious!" agreed Neeve.

Phoebe shrugged. "It's not, really."

"Can you have your friends over for it, too?" asked Kate. She entertained a lot back home, so she was always looking for new party venues. Karaoke carols would be a fun addition to her list of events.

"Melody and Daphne do. I could, but I wouldn't want to. It's too embarrassing," Phoebe winced.

"I think it would be a blast!" said Lark, who had inched over to join in the conversation once she'd realized there wasn't going to be a big family drama.

"Then you haven't seen my dad sing Elvis's 'Blue Christmas' in a Santa hat while my mom and three other nurses from her department sing backup." Phoebe rolled her eyes, but everyone burst out laughing and finally, she had to crack a smile, too.

"Sweetheart! It sounds like your family has a lot of fun traditions! Sure, they're not gathering around a crackling fire to sing 'Silent Night' and drink eggnog, but it still sounds like a good time." Gee looked searchingly at Phoebe.

"I guess," said Phoebe noncommittally.

"Well," said Gee, putting her hands on her knees. "We'll have a different kind of Christmas here this year. We'll make it old-fashioned for you. Then next year, anyone who wants to can come back and we'll do something different."

It sounded like Gee was saying they didn't have to have the plastic stuff on the tree. Phoebe looked up at her hopefully and Gee turned to Neeve. "Neeve, darling, let's let Phoebe do the tree of her dreams this year, since she feels so strongly about it, alright?"

"Sure," agreed Neeve. "Whatever. I don't mind."

"Thank you," said Gee. Phoebe started to stand up, but Gee gestured for her to stay seated. "Now, Phoebe, I'm not letting you off without a tiny lecture. I just can't resist the opportunity!" Gee grinned. "I just want to remind you what I'm sure you already know, which is that Christmas is a celebration that is inclusive and joyful, and the best Christmases are rich in those two qualities, regardless of what your decorations look like. It sounds to me like your parents really make things fun around your house at Christmastime, and they have started some very creative and festive celebrations. They also seem to welcome your friends at every turn, as well as including their own friends and their families. No matter whether you find their traditions 'tacky' or 'embarrassing,' they are your parents and they do love you and try hard to make you happy, especially at Christmastime. So just remember, you could have parents who are completely uptight and rigid about Christmas décor and behavior, so that everything looks right but doesn't feel joyful. And you could have a beautifully decorated house, but no one there but you to admire it." She looked at Phoebe squarely to make sure Phoebe was getting what she was saying.

"I know," said Phoebe. She felt a little ashamed when Gee put it that way.

"I know you do," agreed Gee. "Deep down inside, you do."

Everyone was quiet for a minute, not sure if the lecture was over or not. "Go on, then!" said Gee. "Scoot! Do the tree! I'm going to get a cup of coffee."

Phoebe felt awkward now, and when she went over to the

ornament box, she bent her head so she wouldn't have to meet anyone's eye. But Kate came over to give her a hug, which she endured, and a pat on the shoulder. "Bee, I know how you feel. I take Christmas really seriously, too."

Phoebe nodded. "Thanks." She pulled a little lamb out of the box and straightened its hook, then she looked up at the tree to decide where to place it.

"But listen, I have an idea," continued Kate. Phoebe looked at her, and Kate gestured to Phoebe to come close so she could whisper in her ear. Phoebe looked to see where Neeve, Hillary, and Lark were, but they were engrossed in the box of *Priscilla's* brand chocolates (imported from Cape Cod) on the coffee table, so Phoebe leaned in to hear the secret. As Kate whispered, a smile spread slowly across Phoebe's face, and Phoebe nodded emphatically. "Great idea!" she said, when Kate had finished.

Kate smiled. "Thanks!" And she inched the box of plastic decorations over to the corner so they could use it later.

CHAPTER NINE

Doing for Others

*I*t was nearly dark when they finished the tree, and Phoebe had Neeve plug in the tree lights, while she turned off most of the other lights in the room and then stood with her hand on the light switch for the final two lamps.

"Everyone ready?" asked Phoebe in excitement.

"Yes!" called the girls and Gee in reply, and Phoebe turned off the lights.

There was a collective intake of breath and then a hush fell over the room. The tree looked magical. It was tall and dark against the light walls, with white lights twinkling along its branches, and the muted decorations allowing the natural beauty of the tree to take center stage. It was just what Phoebe had always dreamed of: wonderful, like a tree from another era, and just like the tree on the page of the magazine, but only Phoebe really knew that. Phoebe was proud of her vision and the team effort that had achieved that vision. And she could truly tell herself that it had been a joyful and inclusive process after all. Well, after everyone had agreed to do it her way. But that was okay, there were no hard feelings. And she and Kate had their plan for later just to make sure.

Gee spoke first. "Beautiful, girls. Just beautiful."

"Yeah," agreed Hillary.

"Thanks, everyone," said Phoebe. She studied the tree for a moment longer; what was missing? *Oh!* Something for the top. The angel. Guilt flooded her chest and warmed her face. She glanced at the others to see if they could tell something was amiss with the tree, but no one looked puzzled or disappointed, only pleased. Relieved that no one had said anything, she made a vow that she'd dream up something to replace the angel. Something good.

Phoebe turned the lights back on and the spell was broken. "Should we do the guest list for the party?" she suggested, and everyone agreed.

"Hey? Where's our notebook?" asked Kate. All summer, the cousins had used a big spiral-bound notebook for keeping track of their adventures and plans. The Christmas party and miscellaneous holiday plans (the sleepover, gift lists, etc.) were clearly in need of some organizing, and only the notebook would do.

They quickly determined it was still down in the Dorm, so Hillary borrowed Gee's set of keys from the kitchen and, jamming on her boots and grabbing a flashlight, made a sprint down to the Dorm to retrieve the book.

"Hey!" she said, breathing only a little bit hard when she returned. She tossed the notebook to Phoebe and flopped on the couch. "It's gotten kind of warm out there. The snow's already turning slushy."

"No!" cried Phoebe, flying to the window. "But what about our white Christmas?" She cupped her hands around her eyes to block out the light from inside the living room, and stared out at the yard. It was hard to tell, but the white blanket that had covered the lawn all day was looking a little threadbare. "This is terrible!" Phoebe turned back from the window.

"It is a disappointment, but it's not a surprise, really, sweetheart," said Gee sympathetically. "Snow rarely sticks here. I don't know if it's because of all the salt in the air and on the ground or that we're so exposed to the wind. Also, I think the warm front I read about in the paper might be moving in, too."

Phoebe was let down. She'd been so thrilled by the snow earlier that she'd blocked out Gee's warning about the warm front coming behind it. She'd expected the snow to last all the way through Christmas.

"Let's focus on the party," instructed Neeve, always eager for social diversion. Phoebe came back to sit with the others. At least the party planning would be a good distraction. "Who are we having?"

"Lark," said Hillary, to start. Lark grinned shyly. "And Atticus." Atticus was another pal from Sailing Clinic.

"Talbot," called Neeve.

"And Tessa and Andrea," added Kate.

"Hey, can we ask adults?" Hillary turned to Gee.

"Sure, sweetheart. Whomever you like."

"Okay then, Farren," said Hillary. Farren owned the Little Store, which was the only shop on North Wing, the summer estate section of Gull Island, where Gee's house was. The Little Store sold everything from canned food and dairy stuff to penny candy, beach toys, jewelry, and film. At this time of year, it also sold sleds, Christmas decorations, and candy canes.

Thinking about the party cheered Phoebe up a little. "And Mrs. Merrihew and Mr. Bradshaw," she added. Phoebe loved the librarian and the owner of the local bookstore, and had spent a great deal of time discussing books with them over the summer. "And Sloan," she added quietly, her eyes lowered so she wouldn't have to see anyone's expression. She'd already told Sloan about the party so now they had to invite her, annoying or not.

"And the Hagans," added Neeve. The older couple that ran the marina and sailing school were old friends of Gee's anyway.

"Smitty," said Hillary. Although he was a Bicket, Smitty was more like Sheila than Sloan, and he'd helped them out a lot over the summer by repairing their boat at his shop.

"Hey, should we ask the mayor?" laughed Neeve. The mayor had donated the use of his parking spot in town to be auctioned off at a benefit the girls had worked on over the summer. No one could believe Neeve had had the audacity to ask him to donate it, but he'd been very nice, finding the idea a riot.

"Yes, he's a lovely man," said Gee. "Oh, and put down Father Ryan, please. He'd love to come, I'm sure."

"Too bad Tucker's not around," said Hillary, and everyone sighed in agreement. Their sailing instructor had been a summer lodger at the Bickets, and he had returned to school.

"Lark, dear, I'll give your parents a call, too. I'd love for them to come, and the St. Johns, and even . . . the Bickets." Gee said it briskly, so no one could argue. "I'll call a few of my other friends, too. It will be such fun!" She clapped her hands girlishly.

"Speaking of which, I think it's time for me to go home. I'm just going to go call my dad to come pick me up," announced Lark, standing up.

"Don't be silly, sweetheart," said Gee, standing, too. "I'll drive you. Would anyone like to come for the ride?"

"Sure," agreed Neeve. "And let's stop by the Little Store and invite Farren on our way back."

"Great idea. I'll just get my coat," agreed Gee.

The girls said their goodbyes to Lark, and Hillary went upstairs for a shower. It was the perfect moment for Kate and Phoebe to carry out their little surprise for Neeve. As soon as the door closed behind Gee, Neeve, and Lark, Phoebe and Kate dashed into the kitchen and grabbed the mini-Christmas tree that sat on the sideboard. It was in a terra cotta pot and it stood about two and a half feet high. Sheila looked at them as they carried it, shuffling, back toward the living room, but she just shook her head laughing and didn't ask a thing.

They hefted it onto the coffee table, and then Kate dragged the box of junky ornaments over. It only took about ten minutes total to cover the whole tree, and it was truly covered; hardly an inch of green was visible. There was Fred Flintstone holding a huge leg of what looked like turkey, tied with a red ribbon; Smurfs in elf costumes perched jauntily on branches; Pluto rode a skateboard with a Santa hat on his head; and a troll doll with red and green hair was skewered on the very top, where the angel would go.

After loading it up as quickly as possible, Phoebe and Kate sat back and admired their handiwork.

"It's so cute!" said Kate.

"Disgusting," Phoebe grinned. "But she'll love it, I'm sure. Now let's get the boxes out of here so it looks all clean and set up."

Hillary joined them fresh from her shower. She laughed in surprise at the junky tree and helped them carry the empty boxes back up to the third floor. They were on their last trip up when they heard Gee's car coming up the drive, so they flung the boxes into the attic door, pulled it shut, and raced downstairs to be sure to catch Neeve's reaction.

When the door opened and Gee and Neeve walked in, Kate called, "Yoo-hoo! Come see what we did!"

Neeve walked into the living room with her jacket still on and a look of confusion on her face. But when she spotted the tree, her jaw dropped, and she bent over and put her hands on her knees in shock. "Wow, you guys! It's awesome! Thanks!" Slowly, she stood back up and came to admire their work.

Gee followed behind her, unwinding the scarf from her neck. She, too, looked perplexed until she spotted the tree, then a huge twinkling smile spread across her face. "Lovely!" she said. She sought Phoebe's eyes and when they met, she nodded her head approvingly and sent a wink in Phoebe's direction.

Phoebe beamed. The little tree wasn't her taste at all, but it was nice to see Neeve crouching next to it, laughing and admiring all the funny ornaments.

"Thanks, Bee," said Neeve, smiling up at Phoebe.

"It was Kate's idea, really," said Phoebe.

"Well, thank you both, then," said Neeve, turning back to the tree. "It's just grand."

That night at dinner, Gee asked them each about what kind of charitable or community things they did with their families at Christmastime back home. Kate and her mom baked pies and cookies for soup kitchens, to be distributed on Christmas day. And, no matter where she was, Neeve always spent a day or two at the U.S. Embassy, organizing the Toys for Tots campaign that was invariably taking place. She'd sort presents and wrap them, and then tag them with age and gender information. Hillary and her mom delivered Christmas wreaths and bouquets to people in the hospital; it was part of a program at the Rocky Mountain Hospital, where her mother was a doctor.

Phoebe, who'd been listening intently to the others, cringed when Gee got around the table to her. She was embarrassed that she really had nothing to say.

"Um, we make cards in school for elderly people in nursing homes," she said with an apologetic wince.

"But don't you do anything as a family?" asked Gee, perplexed.

Phoebe shrugged. "Not really. I know my mom and dad do stuff at the hospital, too." Her dad was a doctor and her mom a nurse. "They just always say it's too sad for us kids, so they do it on their own."

"Sad? What on earth?! There's nothing sad about spreading Christmas joy!" said Gee.

"No, but the people are in sad shape, and it's kind of depressing, I guess," said Phoebe. She was confused. Her parents always went off and did their charity work on their own. Phoebe and her sisters weren't part of it, and the reason why, as Phoebe had always understood it, was that the circumstances of the people who were being helped were too dire and sad, and children needed to be protected from being exposed to them, if at all possible. It was like how they weren't allowed to go to funerals yet or something; her parents wanted to preserve her innocence. She'd never really thought about it until this year. Once she realized that she was having a Proper

Christmas, she knew that some kind of charitable work would be part of it. After all, that's what people always did in books and movies: helped other people at Christmastime. She just hadn't figured out what she herself could do.

"I can see what they mean," Gee was saying with a slow nod. "But if you can find an appropriate activity for the family to do all together, it's wonderful. Also, I think it's very important for us to give back, since our family has been very fortunate in life, not just financially — but also in terms of our health and our happiness, and our love for one another, and the fact that none of your dads ever had to go to war, and things like that. We've just been very lucky." She looked around at the girls to make sure they understood her.

"You know, when your fathers were children, we used to have everyone in the family signed up for volunteer work at all times, and not just at Christmas. It was a big thing with Pops; his parents had done the same thing for him and his sisters and brothers, and he insisted that all nine of our children give back to the world. You know the verse from St. Luke in the Bible, 'To whomever much has been given, of him much will be required.'"

Everyone but Phoebe nodded. She shifted uncomfortably in her seat. They didn't talk much about the Bible in her family. "What did our dads do for volunteer work?" asked Phoebe to hide her ignorance.

"Well, you see, they all went to Catholic school, so there was always something organized by the school that you could participate in, like an extracurricular activity. Sometimes it was delivering meals to housebound people, or walking their dogs for them. In the winter, Phoebe, your dad used to shovel snow for some of the elderly people in our neighborhood, which was a wonderful idea that he'd dreamed up all by himself." Phoebe felt warm with pride thinking about her dad doing that as a kid.

"What about my dad?" prompted Kate.

Gee laughed at her eagerness. "Let's see, I think your father did trash pickup at the local park a couple of times a month." Kate wrinkled her nose in distaste. "Oh, and he organized a coat drive at the church one time." Kate visibly preferred that memory.

Gee continued. "And Hillary, I remember your dad selling Christmas trees to benefit the church's soup kitchen. And Neeve, your father used to organize dances in the church basement and then charge people admission and sell baked goods and things, and all the proceeds would go to some overseas charity or another."

Neeve laughed. "So he's always been the same, huh?"

"Always," said Gee, mock-serious.

Hillary laughed. "It sounds just like something you would do, Neeve!"

"You're right," agreed Neeve.

"So, since I moved to Gull full-time a few years ago, I've been participating in a church holiday project that I find very satisfying, because it directly helps people, and you know you're not just throwing things out there and hoping someone who needs them gets them." Gee paused to wipe her mouth with her napkin, and then she continued. "I thought that this year, you girls could help me."

"Yes!" Everyone clamored to agree, even though they had no idea what it was.

Gee smiled. "Every Christmas, Father Ryan gets a list from a parish on the mainland where his friend is the pastor. It's a very poor parish, and the people have few things and even less money to buy the things they need, never mind extras for Christmas. Father Ryan's list has various families on it, and it breaks them down by the ages and genders of the family members, and sometimes even mentions what they might need or want, like a warm jacket or a baby doll. So the members of our church here each take a family and then shop for them. You won't be going into the trenches," said Gee with a wink to Phoebe to show she was joking. "Father Ryan brings it all over on the ferry during the day on Christmas Eve, so the families can get it in time for Christmas morning." Gee looked around the table and was clearly pleased by the eagerness in each of the girls' eyes. She smiled. "We're getting our list tomorrow morning when I go to mass, and I was hoping we could all go to town together and pick out some presents for the family."

"Definitely!" said Phoebe, nodding vigorously. "What an excellent idea!" She was eager to make amends for her lack of charity experience and planned to lead the charge tomorrow, even though she wasn't much of a shopper.

The others agreed.

"So it's settled then. We'll go at ten, right when the shops open."

CHAPTER TEN

Giving

*W*hile Gee was at church the next morning, the girls got dressed, came downstairs, and feasted on Sheila's crumb-topped cinnamon and sour cream coffee cake along with heaps of crispy bacon. Neeve drank her black coffee while Kate grilled Sheila for the coffee cake recipe, and Hillary read the sports pages. Phoebe had her new book with her — a delicious historical novel about a midwife's apprentice in the middle ages — and she was reading with her sock-clad feet drawn up under her on the banquette. The morning weather was disappointing after yesterday's snow. It was strangely foggy and warm, almost like summer, or Florida at this time of year, Phoebe realized morosely, and there was hardly a trace of snow left, save for a few dirty-looking patches here and there. Staring out the window at the damp gray day, Phoebe needed a lift.

She put her book down on the tablecloth, facedown. "What should we make Gee for Christmas?" she asked suddenly.

"Phoebe, I think we've established that no one needs to *make* anything for anyone else for Christmas," said Neeve witheringly. She glared an icy glare at Phoebe until Phoebe met her eyes. Phoebe dipped her head, point taken, and Neeve continued. "I actually brought her a silk robe from Singapore already," said Neeve. "It's pink and I think she'll love it."

Kate nodded. "I was on the Old Mill website this fall and I found this adorable needlepoint pillow with a bunch of pink roses and sweet peas, and all the yarn for it. It looked like Gee. I was going to buy it for her and send it to her, even before I knew we were coming back for Christmas. But if we're going to make stuff, I guess I could always paint a little picture for her or something. . . ." Neeve stared daggers at her, and Kate shrugged innocently.

Hillary announced that she was going to get Gee these new swimming goggles she'd read about. She was sure Booker's would have them because they were apparently the "must have" item for swimmers this year. "Goggles are kind of hard to make," she said with a giggle.

"So what did you have in mind, Mrs. Claus?" Neeve asked Phoebe.

"I don't know. I just feel like it should be something really special. Something memorable, that will be like a big thank you for having us and a memento of our time here with her." Phoebe rested her chin in her hand thoughtfully and stared out the window again. "I just don't want it to be some empty purchase."

Neeve rolled her eyes in exasperation, and Hillary went back to the sports page. But everyone was quiet for a minute, clearly trying to think up something perfect for Gee, homemade or not.

Just then, Gee's car crunched up to the parking area near the back door, and they heard her car door slam. Then the back door opened, making the green curtain billow with air from outside. "Yoo-hoo! Chickadees! I'm home!" Gee announced. The curtain flung open and she appeared, as if onstage. Gee stepped in and lifted her hat off her head. She looked at the girls and smiled. "What's wrong? You all look so serious!"

"Oh. . . ." Kate was a terrible liar, which wasn't a bad quality, when you really thought about it, but they couldn't exactly tell Gee they were thinking about her Christmas present.

Phoebe stepped in. "I was just telling them about my book." She held up the paperback. "It's really dramatic."

"Hmmm," said Gee, squinting across the kitchen at the cover. "Is it good?" She toed off her boots and arranged them neatly by the door so as not to track damp footprints all over the floor.

"Yes!" said Phoebe, so relieved that Gee had taken the bait that her answer came out more forcefully than she'd meant it to. "It's quite good," she added in a tamer voice.

Gee smiled. "You are a terrific reader, Phoebe Callahan.

One of the greatest of all time." She came over and gave Phoebe a pat on the head.

Phoebe beamed. "I love books."

Gee removed a folded sheet of computer paper from her purse and came across the kitchen to join them at the table. She pulled out a chair and sat down. "That's going to be extra handy today, because we seem to have a reader on our list, too."

"Oh, let's see!" squealed Kate eagerly.

"Alright." Gee smoothed the paper out on the table, and Kate came to stand behind Gee so she could look over her shoulder. Gee had put on her glasses and was scanning the list.

"Read it out loud, Katie," commanded Neeve.

"Okay. There are, let's see . . . one, two, three, four, five kids. And a mom. And a grandmother. The kids' ages are two, five, eight, twelve, and fourteen. The mom is thirty-three, and the grandmother is fifty-three. They need . . . some cold-weather clothes, the grandmother would like a warm blanket, the younger kids each want a toy, but the fourteen-year-old wants a book. He's a boy. The ones in the middle are girls and the two-year-old is another boy. It has their clothing sizes here."

The girls were quiet, thinking about the needs of this family they didn't know, and about how lucky they were in comparison, to have everything they needed.

"Gosh," said Hillary.

"It's kind of sad," said Phoebe. "I feel bad for them."

Her imagination started galloping ahead, but Gee interrupted in a businesslike tone. "I'm glad to be reminded once again that you're all compassionate people, but feeling sad about it won't help anyone. You've done nothing to cause their situation, and they don't need you to feel sorry for them. Anyhow, for all you know, they are recent immigrants to this country, and their lives have been significantly improved by their arrival here. Look, they're all together, they're apparently healthy, and they have the resources and know-how to seek help."

Gee was the most caring and charitable person Phoebe knew; she gave her time, her hard work, and plenty of money to lots of important causes. And right now, her eyes were filled with steely determination, which Phoebe tried to draw comfort from.

Gee went on, looking at each of the girls. "Think about what John Bradford said, 'There but for the grace of God, go [I].' It could be any of us one day — although I hope not — leaning on the church for help through a difficult patch." She slapped her hands on the table, palms down. "So. We'll just buy some things, wrap and label them, and we will have been helpful. You just have to keep looking forward and moving forward in life, helping people as much as you can, but not getting bogged down in sadness. Sadness doesn't help anyone."

Phoebe took a deep breath. Gee was right. She'd just move ahead to the idea of the kids opening their presents and think about the joy they'd feel. No more complicated than that. She would do what she could to help.

Neeve bucked up first. "So, where to?" she asked.

"Barefoot Toys, obviously," said Kate.

"Booker's, for the clothes," contributed Hillary.

Phoebe smiled. "Summer Reading."

"The hardware and fabric store has a good housewares section. We can get a blanket there, and a few other things," said Gee.

"What about food?" asked Kate.

"Their church prepares a Christmas dinner. We've tried to send food in the past, but the families are all different ethnicities, and not everyone eats turkey or ham on Christmas the way we do. I usually just make a donation to their food fund when I send in the packages." Gee took off her glasses and let them drop around her neck. "Shall we?" she asked with a grin.

"Yes!" the girls agreed enthusiastically, and they rose to bundle up.

Town was surprisingly busy for this time of year, but it was the last Saturday before Christmas, so probably everyone on the island had at least some shopping to do. They parked in the big central lot by the Bicket Bouquet, Sloan's family's huge grocery store, and crossed the slushy parking lot to enter the back door of Barefoot Toys.

At first, the girls were shy and tentative, almost as if they were the children receiving the gifts. They felt funny about spending too much money, and also wanted to be sure they were choosing appropriately. Phoebe would politely hold up a toy and ask, "Eight-year-old girl?" and the others would nod and look at Gee for her opinion. But Gee encouraged them to go a little crazy, and soon they were zinging around the store, checking and comparing, selecting and then replacing various items.

After about twenty minutes, they settled on a big set of blocks, a large multipack of Hot Wheels, and a huge box of crayons and paper for the two-year-old boy; the five-year-old girl got a Barbie with a few changes of clothes, a soccer ball, and a neat board game. For the eight-year-old girl, they chose a craft kit filled with beads, a set of Hello Kitty colored pencils, stickers and paper, and a game pack that had cards, jacks, and tiddlywinks. The twelve-year-old girl got a pink CD player and radio cube, a little camera and scrapbook with stuff to decorate the pages, and a make-your-own-perfume kit. The fourteen-year-old boy got a cool skateboard and a Game Boy that came with three games, and they'd add in some books for everyone when they got to Summer Reading.

The girls were giddy when they finished. It was weird but kind of fun shopping for strangers, trying to imagine what might make them happy on Christmas morning. The girls agreed that they themselves would be happy with each of the presents, if they were the ages of those kids, and they were pleased when the store offered to wrap and label everything for them. They could return with the car when they'd finished their other shopping, and one of the store clerks would bring everything out to them.

"Wow! That was fun!" said Phoebe, as they left through the front door and headed down the sidewalk to Booker's.

"I love that place," agreed Hillary.

The snow in town had become big gray puddles at each curb, and the water sloshed back and forth as though it had an undertow; the girls were glad Gee had told them to wear boots. The smell of the soaked mulch in the Christmas tree planters mingled with the aroma of cinnamon donuts from the News Co., and the cozy smell of wood smoke united the scents to make it smell like a late fall afternoon. Despite the gray day, everyone on the street seemed happy, and even strangers smiled at the girls as they walked along.

"'*It's beginning to look a lot like Christmas!*'" sang Neeve, somewhat tunelessly, but in a loud voice.

"'*Everywhere we go!*'" added Kate, her beautiful soprano joyful and clear in the foggy, wet air.

Phoebe was a little embarrassed at them making a spectacle of themselves, but when she saw Gee laugh, Phoebe's shame quickly turned to joy. Why shouldn't they share their happiness with the world, anyway? she thought, suddenly inspired by Gee's example. They were healthy, all together, lucky, fed, and warm, and it was Christmastime. And what was more Christmassy than celebrating your happiness on a cool day in a cozy New England town? Phoebe gave a little skip, her hands nestled in her pockets.

She turned to look in the window of the post office and saw a big, colorful poster advertising something called "A Christmas Walk." She paused while the others walked ahead, and read that Sunday night, tomorrow, all the stores would stay open late and there would be "Seasonal Festivities," and the shopping streets closed to traffic, for a winter celebration. Certain proceeds would go to charity. She skipped ahead to catch up with the others, and mentioned the poster to Gee.

"Yes! I can't believe I forgot to tell you! We'll definitely come out for it. It's wonderful. You'll see."

The cousins pressed Gee for details and she described carolers in old-fashioned costumes, roasted marshmallows and other treats, giveaways and mini-sales in every store, horse-drawn carriage rides, and more. Phoebe was excited. It sounded like something out of a novel.

When they reached Booker's, it was bustling and Talbot was there, thrilled to see them, with big hugs all around, even for Gee. The store had set up a keg of hot cider with paper cups, for their shoppers, and all the girls had some while they chatted with Talbot and invited him to their Christmas party. And then it was time again to shop.

This time, the girls were less shy. Their section of the counter was quickly heaped with mittens, hats, and scarves. They added turtlenecks and long underwear, and three-packs of warm wool socks. Then Gee decided to splurge and bought a fleece jacket for everyone in the Christmas charity family — gorgeously soft and brightly colored, all different: hot pink, rich garnet, royal blue, deep forest green, gold, and more. Kate actually clapped at the sight of them and Phoebe laughed.

The store was too busy to wrap everything, so they slid folded gift boxes into the shopping bags, and tissue and stretchy ribbons, and Phoebe and Hillary carried the bags to the car while Gee paid and Neeve and Kate talked with Talbot again. They'd meet up afterward at the hardware store.

Walking around the corner to the parking lot, Hillary was plotting out loud about when she could get back to Booker's to buy the goggles for Gee. (They had had them, of course.) But Phoebe stopped suddenly in her tracks. She'd caught sight of another colorful poster hanging on a wall with some other flyers, and she was staring at it, frozen like a statue.

Hillary stopped, too, laughing. "Phoebe, you just can't pass by the written word, can you? You have to read absolutely everything!"

Phoebe smiled distractedly. It was an ad for "Christmas Puppies." Golden retrievers, eight weeks old tomorrow. There was a digital photo in the middle of the flyer, and the bottom of the page had been sliced into tear-off ribbons, each with a local phone number. All of her life, Phoebe had wanted a golden retriever puppy. Especially for Christmas. Every year she would dutifully put it on her Christmas list, until it became kind of a family joke. Her mom wasn't crazy about big dogs living indoors, and she always argued that the girls were too young to help take care of a dog. With both parents working so much, who would walk it and feed it?

But Phoebe thought the best Christmas present in the world had to be a puppy of your very own, with a red bow around his neck, tearing around the living room on Christmas morning. Without thinking, she reached out, tore one of the little tabs from the poster, and put it in her coat pocket.

Hillary smiled. "Those little guys remind me of Winnie when he was a baby." Winnie was her golden, named after Winnie the Pooh when she was five. "Goldens are such good dogs. They love you and like to cuddle, but they're also really athletic and superprotective of their owners. I'll always have one."

They'd reached the car. Phoebe lifted the tailgate and they placed the bags inside. Then they continued across the parking lot to cut through to Broad Street and cross over to the hardware store.

"I wonder why Gee doesn't have any pets," said Phoebe.

"Well, she travels a lot," said Hillary.

"But Sheila's always around."

"I think they used to have lots of pets when our dads were growing up. Maybe when the kids all moved out she just never got any new pets."

"Yeah."

They reached Broad Street just as Gee and the others were coming around the corner. They all crossed together and headed into the hardware store, where they quickly snapped up a fuzzy blanket with silky trim, and six down sleeping bags, "just in case their house isn't warm enough," said Gee. The owner left everything by the door in bags, and the Callahans would pick them up when they drove past later.

Then it was time for Summer Reading. Phoebe's heart lifted in anticipation of a visit to her favorite bookstore. She was a tiny bit shy about seeing Mr. Bradshaw again, but she was looking forward to visiting the store and finding out what was new. She also loved the idea of shopping there for someone else.

CHAPTER ELEVEN

Guardian Angels

There were sleigh bells hanging on a leather strap on the door, so when they opened it to enter, it sounded like Santa was arriving. Inside, Ella Fitzgerald was crooning Christmas carols over the sound system, and the smell of pine was so rich it was like being inside a forest. On a table just inside the door to the right, there was a huge jar of red and white peppermints, free for the taking, and all kinds of wrapping paraphernalia — ribbons, bows, gift tags, wrapping paper — all for the store to wrap your books beautifully, while you waited.

The familiar smell of cinnamon coffee wafted through the air, and ahead to the left, where the store rose up to a cathedral ceiling, was a massive Christmas tree, hung with all sorts of minibooks as decorations, and tiny white paper angels blowing trumpets. There were shoppers all around, and people sitting in the cozy armchairs, scarves and jackets opened, with books in their laps and shopping bags at their feet. It was hard to tell if people were more interested in shopping for themselves, as a little holiday reward, or for gifts for others.

Mr. Bradshaw was over in the children's section, just finishing up with a baffled-looking grandfather type. The girls and Gee proceeded in his direction, since it was where they'd need to do the bulk of their shopping. As they were halfway across the store, he turned and saw them coming, and gave a surprised smile and a big wave.

"Well, if it isn't the Callahan cousins! And their grandmother! Merry Christmas! How are you, girls? Welcome back!"

Gee greeted him warmly; she'd been in the store often over the fall, and they also saw each other regularly at various town functions. The other girls said hello and Phoebe explained why they were there, and she and Mr. Bradshaw fell into deep discussion about what would be appropriate book choices for a fourteen-year-old boy. Mr. Bradshaw suggested they head over to the Classic Literature section.

Phoebe and Mr. Bradshaw worked quickly; they both knew the inventory quite well. They made a little pile, and when the stack had grown to ten paperbacks, Phoebe reviewed it. "Okay, so we're doing *Lonesome Dove, Moby Dick, Last of the Mohicans, Norton Anthology of Poetry*. . . ." Mr. Bradshaw went to grab a dictionary and a thesaurus as well, and then he and Phoebe agreed that it was quite a wonderful collection of books, and he took the pile off to the register to add up and have one of his clerks start wrapping.

The others were gathered in a little knot by the board books, debating the virtues of *Goodnight Moon* versus *Guess How Much I Love You.* Phoebe went to take a spin past the gardening section, to see if there was anything she could buy Gee for Christmas if it came to that, but she was blocked from this direction by a big display of angel books. At every turn she was reminded of the angel of Gee's that she'd destroyed! She'd never get over it. And of all things, she really couldn't stand angels. She sighed out loud and detoured.

A few more decisions were made, and then the girls and Gee all went up to the counter. Phoebe hadn't been inspired by the selection of gardening books, but she couldn't tell if it was her mood (she hated to give in that quickly on the homemade gift question) or that the choices were lousy. She'd have to come back another time.

Up at the counter, there were little display piles of gift books — last-minute stocking stuffer ideas and impulse buys. Gee picked up a book and flipped through it, then she added it to their pile, and Kate and Neeve each selected little books and began reading snippets aloud to each other. Hillary wandered over to the bulletin board near the door — she had probably had enough and was itching to get outside — but just seconds later, Hillary pulled something from the board and came loping back to Phoebe instead.

She held a little piece of paper in her outstretched hand. "Here," she said, offering it to Phoebe.

"What is it?" asked Phoebe.

"The golden puppies again," said Hillary, grinning.

Phoebe rolled her eyes. "Thanks," she said, taking the little tab and rolling it up into a ball before she shoved it in her pocket.

But Mr. Bradshaw had overheard them. "That's our dog — our other dog, I should say. Really my wife's dog. The puppies are so darn cute — you can hold them in one hand. And they're soft as silk." He was taking the wrapped books from a sales clerk and placing them in shopping bags.

Gee and the cousins listened with interest. "How old are they?" asked Gee politely.

"Just about eight weeks. Want one?" he winked at Gee to show he was joking.

"Heavens, no," said Gee. "But I do love goldens. We had a great one when the kids were growing up. They're such terrific company, and so gentle with children."

"Very loyal, too," said Mr. Bradshaw. "If my wife and I ever argue, her dog goes right to her side and barks at me if I raise my voice."

Gee laughed. "I could've used a dog like that once or twice in my marriage!"

Mr. Bradshaw laughed and gave Gee the total for the sale, and Gee handed him her credit card. While he slid her card through the machine on the table behind the register, he turned over his shoulder and said, "Our golden saved one of the kids' lives, one time, too. I'm sure of it."

"Oh my. What happened?" asked Gee in concern.

"It was a scene right out of *Lassie*," said Mr. Bradshaw, referring to an old television show about a heroic dog. "Our oldest, Max, was climbing a tree out in the side yard, and he fell and was knocked unconscious. . . ."

Gee gasped. "Oh dear!"

"And Maggie came running up to the house, barking up a storm, and wouldn't let up until she'd gotten Sally down the hill and out to where Max was lying on the ground."

"He was okay, though . . . ," said Gee.

"Yes, of course. He woke up and Sally took him down to the clinic. He had a concussion — nothing much you can do about it, but they did have us wake him all night long to make sure he was okay." Mr. Bradshaw turned with Gee's receipt for her to sign.

Gee lifted her glasses on their chain and perched them on her nose. "Goodness, that is scary! You might never have known!"

"Right! Max might have come to, walked around all day with a concussion, gone to bed that night and never woken up again."

"Oh, don't even say it!" said Gee, removing her glasses. "I hope Maggie got a nice piece of steak for dinner that night."

Mr. Bradshaw laughed. "You bet she did! And every night for about a month after!"

"Good for her!" said Gee. She put her credit card back into her purse and clipped it shut. "Well, John, thanks for your help with everything! And good luck with the goldens!"

The girls gathered up the bags and everyone headed for the door, calling goodbye to Mr. Bradshaw.

"Let me know if you change your mind about the puppies!" he called after them, and Gee laughed.

The sleigh bells went *jink, jink, jink* as they left the store, and the damp air outside swirled around them, lifting Phoebe's hair and blowing Gee's pink scarf all aflutter.

"Why don't I go get the car and you girls can wait here with the books?" suggested Gee.

"How about if I run ahead to Barefoot Toys to tell them we're coming, and then I'll wait for you outside?" suggested Hillary.

"We can grab the bags from the hardware store and meet you outside of there," added Neeve.

"I'll stay here with the books," offered Phoebe, gesturing to the park bench outside the store. Usually it was filled with readers perusing their new purchases, but today it was empty. People were just too busy.

"Perfect. Thanks, sweethearts," said Gee, and she left, crossing over Broad Street to cut through to the parking lot.

Phoebe hefted the shopping bag onto the bench beside her and looked around. *Darn!* she thought. *Why didn't I bring something to read?* It was unlike Phoebe to ever be caught without a book, but she hadn't expected to need one during their shopping trip. She peered into the bag next to her, but everything was gift-wrapped. Except . . . what was that, down in the corner? Oh, the little gift book Gee bought.

Phoebe reached down into the depths of the bag, trying not to rip its sides. She scrabbled around until she caught hold of the book, and she fished it out for a look.

"Blast!" she yelled, and dropped the book back into the bag as if she'd been burned. It was a book about Christmas angels. Would she *never* escape them? Realizing how loudly she'd shouted, Phoebe looked around shyly, but no one had noticed. Darn it. Worse than nothing to read! Something bad to read!

She drummed her fingers on the bench and stared up and down the street, willing Gee's Volvo to appear around the corner. But the roads were crowded today — probably lots of people picking up shopping and holiday supplies — and traffic was only inching along the two streets.

In exasperation, Phoebe lifted her hands and redid the bun in her hair. And finally, "Oh for Lord's sake!" she blurted. And she fished the book back out again and opened to page one.

CHAPTER TWELVE

The Idea

"*The most wonderful gift I've ever been given is the gift of my first grandchild, and I've been given it twice. . . .*" began the first story. Phoebe nearly gagged at the overly dramatic writing and the cheesy decorative illustrations — angels with wings made of stained glass, cherubs with exaggerated baby faces — all rosy cheeks and blue eyes and red lips. But she was just bored enough to read on. The truth was, she'd even read a jar of mayo if that's all there was.

And slowly, one by one, the stories grabbed her. They weren't long and they weren't polished, but they were heartfelt and grateful and they were all supposedly true. Phoebe, who never ever cried, felt her eyes well up once or twice as she quickly read through the minibook of heartbreak and healing. *Phoebe Callahan!* She reprimanded herself. *Get control of yourself! This isn't Jane Austen! It's the . . . Dorito of the book world. It's fluffy cotton candy compared to a multivitamin. It's wasting space in your brain! Stop! Stop reading it!* But she couldn't. She was hooked. So hooked in fact, that when Gee's car pulled up on the opposite side of the street to pick her up, she didn't even hear Gee calling her. Gee ended up cruising on to the end of the road, u-turning, and coming back to pull up alongside her. She honked this time, and Hillary yelled out the window, and Phoebe snapped out of her reverie. And in doing so she realized she was on the second-to-last story and she was dying for more.

"Oh!" she said guiltily, as if she'd been caught doing something bad. "I was just, um." Flustered, she dropped the book into Gee's shopping bag. All she could think of was how could she get more angel books. Then she remembered the display in the store.

"Gee . . . I'm going to run back in for just one minute, okay? Here, let me just load this in the back like so." She stowed the book in the cargo area and slammed the tailgate shut. "I won't be more than a minute. I'll run up to meet you at the hardware store, okay?"

Gee looked confused and slightly concerned about the manic gleam in Phoebe's eyes, but she agreed and Phoebe hightailed it back into the store. Quickly, she made her way to the display, grabbed the three thickest books in the display (one said "#1 *New York Times* Bestseller!" on it, which would formerly have disgusted Phoebe, who felt that the general public had no taste. But now she understood why it had sold so well. You just couldn't get enough of this stuff. And once you started, the only thing you wanted to do was buy the book for your friends and families so that everyone could have their own copy!).

Nearly breathless with speed and excitement, Phoebe raced up to the checkout, dropped the books on the counter, and waited for the salesgirl to give her the total. While she waited, she thought about the stories she'd read: an angel who saves a woman's grandson from drowning in a pond while he's skating on Christmas eve; the angel who comes to tell the woman that her Marine officer daughter is safe in the Middle East and about to come home for good; the man who nearly gets in a car crash by driving off a closed bridge, but the angel steps in front of his car to save him, telling him his parents are waiting for him on the other side but that his young family needs him on earth for now and many Christmases to come. It went on and on, and each story filled Phoebe with a kind of joy she'd never known.

The thing was, Phoebe was truly a worrywart. But not the kind that Kate was, where she worried about spiders or sharks or muggers. She was worried about bigger things, things that couldn't be explained away, like: *What happens after you die?* and *Why do children starve?* and things like that. True, she'd read too many books that were far too mature for her, and they'd probably poisoned her mind, making her anxious about things kids shouldn't have to worry about. She read the newspapers and news magazines like *Time* and *Newsweek,* and she looked at CNN online. She just had too much information in her mind about the things that could go wrong, and it was very stressful walking around with all the fear and anxiety that that information created in her. That was part of why she didn't cry all that much; little stuff just didn't seem worthy of tears; not when there were malaria epidemics and tsunamis in the world.

But suddenly, these angel stories were giving her relief and comfort, and most of all, hope; and it seemed like these stories were something she'd been seeking for years. Maybe it was just that the timing was right: She was in a super-Christmassy mode and more open to sentimentality than usual. Or maybe it was because she'd seen that Gee sort of liked angels, and that made her realize they weren't just for brain-dead people. Whatever it was, they struck the right chord for the first time, and she was happy.

Phoebe took her change, thanked the cashier, and practically skipped out the door. But it was then that she stopped dead in her tracks and had a thunderbolt of a brainstorm. For on the poster of the golden retrievers that Hillary had pulled the tab from earlier was the headline: "Guardian Angels: Yours for the taking!" And Phoebe realized she'd found the perfect Christmas present for Gee.

▲

Gee had taken the girls home to drop them off with all of the presents for the Christmas family, but she needed to head back to town to do a few errands of her own. The girls volunteered to wrap the remaining unwrapped presents, and she accepted, leaving them with the bags on the front doorstep and a jaunty wave out the car window.

Phoebe had been silent on the drive home, and now she could feel Kate looking at her curiously. She hadn't said anything because she felt like once she started talking, she might not stop. Her head was swimming with angels and angel stories, and most importantly, her present idea for Gee. But she couldn't exactly talk about the dog in front of Gee.

"Where should we do this?" Neeve was asking as they hauled the bags into the front hall.

"Living room," said Kate breathlessly. It wouldn't be so far to carry them.

The girls took a left and began piling the bags in the center of the room on the rug. Phoebe had been thinking of doing some kind of hand-printed wrapping paper — maybe brown craft paper with stamped red stars on it — but then she'd seen the big bag of wrapping paper from the hardware store and realized her idea wasn't even worth mentioning. It wasn't worth fighting for when there were so many other important things to discuss. Still, she'd definitely make her own paper for her presents for the cousins and Gee and Sheila, or at least make her own gift cards.

Kate went to get scissors and Scotch tape from the kitchen, and everyone else settled on the floor. Neeve started doling out things to wrap. Once everyone was seated and had their supplies arrayed around them, Phoebe cleared her throat in a formal fashion.

"Ahem. Guys. I know what to get Gee for Christmas," she said definitively.

Neeve arched one eyebrow and shot Phoebe a look. "Oh, so we're not making anything this year, are we?" she said in a sarcastic voice.

Phoebe narrowed her eyes to give Neeve a dirty look. "In addition to something I might *make,* I found the perfect thing to *get* for her in town."

"What?" Kate was excited, Phoebe was happy to see.

Phoebe looked around to make sure everyone was paying close enough attention. She drew herself upright and calmly said, "A golden retriever puppy."

"Oooh! What a cute idea!" squealed Kate, clapping her hands.

But Neeve and Hillary didn't look as excited.

"What?" challenged Phoebe. "Why isn't it the best idea you've ever heard?" She refused to let them disappoint her.

"Well . . . you can't just give someone a *dog* . . . ," began Hillary diplomatically. "It's kind of like giving someone a kid. It's a lot of work and responsibility."

"I think it's a terrible idea," said Neeve, shaking her head. "Gee travels a lot, and what would she do with a dog while she was away?"

Phoebe had already thought of this. "Sheila could take care of him!"

"It's not really right to just dump a dog on Sheila," said Neeve. "We don't even know if she likes dogs. And anyway, I think Sheila goes home for a month every year, too."

"Then he could stay with someone else — maybe Mr. Bradshaw's wife would keep him when Gee and Sheila were both away. It couldn't be for long. They wouldn't just leave this house by itself for more than a week." Phoebe was frustrated. Couldn't they see that the gift of a dog was so special and exciting that the recipient wouldn't care about details? They'd just figure that stuff out later, once they'd already fallen in love with the little creature.

"I don't know," said Hillary. "That's expecting a lot of other people."

"I can't believe the lack of enthusiasm here, people! It's the best present ever! Wouldn't you love to come down on Christmas morning to find your very own adorable puppy with a big red bow around his neck?" Phoebe folded her arms and jutted out her chin in a challenging pose.

"Oh yes!" agreed Kate.

"Well, I *have* a dog," said Hillary.

"I like dogs fine, but I would not want the responsibility myself," Neeve stated.

"You're just saying that to bolster your argument!" accused Phoebe. "Think with your heart for a second and not with your head." (This was something she'd just picked up from the angel book, and it had already come in handy!) "Wouldn't you be thrilled, emotionally, if it happened to you? Forget about the details. Wouldn't you?"

"What does bolster mean?" asked Kate, but Phoebe ignored her.

"I guess," said Neeve, sighing to show she was giving in.

Phoebe knew she had a toehold now. "Ha! I knew it!" She slapped her knee in satisfaction.

Kate was looking at Phoebe closely. She could feel Kate's eyes on her. "What?" said Phoebe, bristling defensively.

Kate paused, and then she said, "I think *you're* the one who wants a dog. Like, for *you!*"

"Don't be ridiculous!" scoffed Phoebe. "I'm not allowed to have a dog." She looked away.

"That has nothing to do with wanting one," teased Neeve in a singsong voice. "You're totally right," she said, turning to Kate. "Good call!"

Phoebe was irritated. This was undermining her plan. "Regardless of what I want or don't want, I'd like to take a vote on the idea of getting a puppy for Gee. All in favor, raise your hand."

Kate and Phoebe both raised their hands. Hillary said, "If you ask Sheila if she likes dogs and she says yes, then yes. I think it's fine."

"Great! That's a majority!" said Phoebe.

"I guess I don't have a choice then," said Neeve. "Do whatever you like."

Phoebe jumped up to go search out Sheila. There was no time to waste!

"Sheila!" called Phoebe as she walked down the long hall toward the kitchen.

"In here, luv!" called Sheila.

Phoebe entered the kitchen and saw Sheila busy at the counter baking. The KitchenAid standing mixer was in front of her and she was adding ingredients to the batter for something or other. Phoebe had never been hugely into cooking or baking or anything, but this Christmas, she was quite interested to try her hand at some Christmas recipes.

"Yum. What are you making?" asked Phoebe.

"Another of my sour cream coffee cakes," said Sheila. "They go quick at this time a'year, and Mrs. Callahan likes to have 'em around for visitors and for family breakfast. They're dead easy to make," she added.

Phoebe rested her arms on the counter and peered into the bowl while Sheila recited the recipe from memory. It didn't sound hard. "Hey, those would be fun to make and give away to some of our friends," said Phoebe. She was envious of Kate's holiday baking back home and had been meaning to flip through her file and come up with a comparable thing to do here on Gull. Granted, they didn't have as many people to make them for as she would back home, but that would actually make it easier. Six or eight coffee cakes to deliver . . . fun!

"Ya know what're cute?" said Sheila. She wiped her hands on her apron and squatted to rummage in the cabinet under the island. A moment later she rose with a handful of mini-loaf pans. "They make smaller cakes, but they're jest darling. Taste the same, but something about 'em being small. Like tea cakes. People love 'em. I've got about sixteen of 'em, from a project your aunt Kathy did in school one year. Lord knows we never get rid of anything 'round here."

Phoebe took the pans into her hands and looked at them. "Great idea, Sheila! So, if we wanted to make a bunch of these, could you help figure out the recipe? Ingredient quantities and things?"

"Sure, and I'll even help ya's if you'd like," said Sheila with a grin.

"Thanks!" said Phoebe, and she started back toward the living room. But then she smacked her forehead. She'd forgotten the whole reason she'd come in.

"Sheila, do you like dogs?" she asked, trying to make the question sound casual. She was practically cringing as she asked. What if Sheila said no? Then what?!

"Love 'em," Sheila said definitively.

"Woo hoo!" cheered Phoebe, and with her fist in the air, she did a victory jog back to the living room. As she walked, she fished for the Bradshaws' phone number in the pocket of her jeans, nervous now. What if someone else had already taken the puppies? Then what??

CHAPTER THIRTEEN

The Call

$\mathcal{G}$ee came home laden with parcels, and she shooed the girls away when they offered help. "Off you go! I can't have any snooping!" she teased. "Just send Sheila out and then you girls stay in the kitchen. Thanks!"

The girls scrambled into the kitchen and got Sheila. And while Kate, Neeve, and Hillary stood there trying to guess what Gee could possibly have bought for them, Phoebe darted up the back stairs to use the phone in one of the guest rooms.

Nervously, she dialed the Bradshaws' number, and listened to it ring. Her stomach was doing flip-flops and her heart was thudding in her ears, but she was excited, too.

"Hello?" said a woman's voice.

"Um, hi, is . . . Mrs. Bradshaw there, please?" asked Phoebe.

"Speaking," said the woman.

"Oh, hi, um, this is Phoebe Callahan, I'm a . . . customer

of the bookstore, and . . . um . . . I'm interested in your puppies." *Phew!* She'd gotten it out.

"Wonderful!" said Mrs. Bradshaw, and Phoebe breathed a sigh of relief. "We've got a couple of little ones left, and they're just so cute. Is it for you?"

"Yes, um, I mean, it's for my grandmother," said Phoebe.

"That's great! Well, would you like to arrange a time to come see them?"

"Yes. Um, what would be good for you?" asked Phoebe politely.

"How about tomorrow morning? Say, around ten?"

Phoebe agreed and took down the address. They finished up and were hanging up when Mrs. Bradshaw said, "Okay then, I'll see you and your grandmother tomorrow morning at ten then. Bye!" And she hung up.

Uh-oh, thought Phoebe, as she slowly replaced the receiver in its cradle. Obviously, she had no plans to bring Gee with her. After all, it was going to be a surprise. But it was suddenly occurring to her that Mrs. Bradshaw probably would not let a kid just take a dog as a surprise gift for someone. It was like when Kate wanted to get her ears pierced; she'd needed an adult to go with her to give permission.

She sat very still and drummed her hands on the bedside table. Hmm. Maybe she could say she was just coming to check out the puppies and Gee didn't have time to come, too, since she was so busy with Christmas and all. But no, because if Mr. Bradshaw saw Gee and said something about the dog, well, the secret would be ruined. Maybe she could have her mom call and give permission. Ha! Her mother, Mrs. A-Dog-Is-A-Huge-Responsibility, would never do that. She'd say Phoebe had to check with Gee herself first.

Now Phoebe really had to stop and face the truth. And the truth was this: She knew that if Gee found out about the dog ahead of time, she'd say she didn't want it. But Phoebe knew that if she could just get the dog into Gee's hands, then Gee would fall in love with it and want to keep it. But how? And what would she say to the Bradshaws in the meantime? Blast! It was all so frustrating.

"Phoebe! Church!" called Neeve up the back stairs. They always went to five fifteen mass on Saturday nights when they were on Gull. Gee found it easier to "rally the troops" in the late afternoon than first thing Sunday morning, and she always took them out for dinner afterward. It was a family tradition.

Slowly, Phoebe got to her feet. She was deep in thought as she trudged down the hall. But she met the others on their way up the stairs and was confused. "Aren't we going to church?"

"Yes, but we're going to Coolidge House afterward for dinner, so we need to look nicer," said Kate. In the summer they always went to Cabot's Clam Shack after church, so they didn't really need to dress up, but it was closed at this time of year; it was too cold to eat dinner on a covered dock.

Phoebe did a U-turn and followed the others back to their rooms. The three cousins were chattering about what Gee might have bought for them for Christmas, speculating about sporting gear and clothing, but Phoebe didn't participate. She was preoccupied by her problem.

When they separated at the doors to their rooms, Phoebe followed Hillary in, and perched on the edge of her bed, her cheek resting on her hand as she stared at the floor. Hillary was rifling though her suitcase, which she had still not unpacked, looking for something dressy to wear that wasn't totally wrinkled.

"Earth to Phoebe," she said.

"Hmm? Oh. Sorry," said Phoebe.

"Did you call the Bradshaws?" asked Hillary quietly.

"Mmm-hmm."

"And?"

"She was really nice," said Phoebe.

"But?"

"No buts," said Phoebe. She turned to look at Hillary. "Why do you say 'but'?"

"Because there's a but in your voice," said Hillary, laughing.

Phoebe laughed, too, happy to be known so well. "I guess there is," she admitted.

"So?" prodded Hillary.

"I'm going to need an adult's permission," said Phoebe.

Hillary's eyes widened. "They said that?"

"No, but she knows it's for Gee, and she thinks Gee is bringing me tomorrow."

"Oh."

"Yeah," said Phoebe. Phoebe could tell by the expression

on Hillary's face that she knew this was bad news. Slowly, Phoebe stood and went to the closet to select a long, embroidered velvet peasant skirt from the neat row of clothing she'd hung as soon as she'd arrived.

The two roommates were quiet as they dressed, each mulling over the problem. Finally, Hillary said, "Well, what if you just tell them the deal. Be honest. And then see what they say."

Phoebe wasn't sure. If she told them the truth, that she was taking one of their puppies for someone who may or may not want it, they probably wouldn't let her have it. She wouldn't, if she was them.

"They'll say no, is what they'll say," said Phoebe, sliding a long-sleeved red tunic over her head.

"Who will say no?" said Neeve, stepping into the room. Phoebe looked at her and giggled. Neeve had on a saucy little red felt miniskirt trimmed in fake white fur; it was like the skirt version of Santa's cap. On top, Neeve had added a white turtleneck, a gold necklace made of oodles of different-sized interlocking hoops, and she had her hair in tiny stick-out ponytails on either side of her head.

"Cute," said Phoebe.

Neeve spun in a little circle, holding the skirt out with her hands. "Thanks. I made it," she said.

Hillary turned around and laughed. "Are you sure that's appropriate for church?" she asked.

Neeve flounced the skirt and sat down huffily on the bed. "God doesn't care what I wear, as long as I show up."

"But Gee might care," snorted Hillary.

"Gee will love it." Neeve was immovable. "Now what were you talking about when I came in?"

The girls explained the situation, and Kate wandered in halfway through and they reexplained. Finally, when everyone had the facts, Neeve said that Phoebe should just drop the whole idea. Giving Gee a dog without her knowing was just not going to work out, and she wanted no part of it. But when Phoebe began to get upset, Hillary interrupted and proposed that Phoebe just tell the Bradshaws the truth, and see if they would let her have the dog for a couple of days to see what happened. They could think of it as a dog-sitting assignment.

Phoebe agreed to mull over that plan, and they all went downstairs to find Gee.

Church was fine, but Coolidge's was marvelous, Phoebe thought. Just right. The decorations were completely over the top: The wood-paneled and very formal main dining room was decorated to within an inch of its life. There were real pine garlands everywhere and red-and-green plaid taffeta tablecloths that draped and pooled over the tables like ball gowns. Mini pine trees in pots were draped with strings of red and gold beads, popcorn and cranberry chains, and red bows, green bows, gold bows.

Fruit, pinecones, and nuts that had been spray-painted gold were all arranged into beautiful still lifes on mantels and tabletops. And the Christmas tree in the lobby was huge — like the one they'd bought for The Sound — and all decorated with white lights and dozens and dozens of different kinds of seashells that had been spray-painted gold and hung with green and red ribbons. Scads of candles flickered on the dining tables, side tables, and mantels, and it was warm, bright, and noisy in the big, main dining room. As far as Phoebe could see, everyone looked cheerful: bright-eyed and rosy-cheeked and happy.

She was happy, until halfway through her bowl of lobster bisque, when she spotted the Bradshaws entering the dining room. She nearly choked as she simultaneously stepped on Neeve's toe to get her attention.

"Ow!" said Neeve noisily. Luckily Gee was deep in conversation with Kate and Hillary about an artist they all knew who lived in town, so she didn't hear Neeve's outburst.

Phoebe gasped out the words "Look! Help!" and Neeve followed her glance until she spied the Bradshaws. Neeve's eyes widened in a satisfyingly shocked way, but it didn't do any good. The Bradshaws had spotted the Callahans and were now on their way over to say hi. Phoebe was paralyzed; her mind had gone blank and her mouth had dried up. Gee was going to find out.

But Neeve acted fast; and for this, Phoebe would be eternally grateful. She popped up from her seat, excusing herself to go to the bathroom, then she purposely walked toward the Bradshaws, even though it was in the opposite direction from where she needed to go. Gee was still distracted, so she didn't notice Neeve going out of her way to say hello to them, and

Neeve managed to stop them just ten feet short of the Callahans' table and say something quickly and quietly to the Bradshaws, who nodded their heads in agreement. Neeve then did a U-turn and made her pointless trip to the bathroom, and the Bradshaws continued on to the Callahans' table to say hello.

Phoebe was sinking in her chair in dread, but Mr. Bradshaw was smiling and he came over and patted her shoulder and winked at her, then introduced her to Mrs. Bradshaw, who, bless her heart, acted like she'd never even heard of Phoebe Callahan before. Phoebe was so panicked by the interaction that she said nothing, and smiled in a sort of grimace as the Bradshaws chatted briefly with Gee, then continued on to their table.

Neeve returned from the bathroom only seconds later, and Phoebe stared at her in mute relief, but with a question in her eyes.

"Don't worry. I took care of everything," said Neeve under her breath. "I'll tell you later."

"Thanks," sighed Phoebe. *Maybe this whole dog idea wasn't such a good one, after all,* she thought despondently.

CHAPTER FOURTEEN

Puppies!

It was hours before they were all alone again. After dinner, they'd played Scrabble with Gee in the sewing room and discussed the Christmas party plan. Gee was going to hire a few people to come and help Sheila with the serving and cleaning up, and she was going to have Callie's Cupboard in town make some of the hors d'oeuvres and the *bouche de Noël,* so Sheila wouldn't be swamped. There was also liquor to order, and silverware to polish. The tablecloths and napkins needed to be brought down in their tissue (Gee still sent them to her old cleaner in Boston to carefully wash and iron, since they were antique Irish linen and very delicate).

Phoebe was very excited by the party plans. She was looking forward to a big, fancy holiday party — unlike the untraditional and casual karaoke parties back home, where everyone wore jeans and ate sushi. The plans distracted her for a good while, but eventually she started getting antsy to find out what

Neeve had said to the Bradshaws. And while she usually loved Scrabble (she was excellent at it and really enjoyed playing with Gee, who was also excellent), tonight she found it slow and a little too long.

Just as they were wrapping it up — Gee had scored 120 on a triple word score — Sheila came in to say goodnight, and reminded Phoebe about the mini-coffee cakes.

"Oh! Right!" said Phoebe, newly animated with excitement. And she quickly explained her holiday baking plan to the others.

Gee had been quiet during Phoebe's explanation. Phoebe assumed she was totaling everyone's scores, but then she said, "I was just thinking. You know, we're having a Christmas bazaar at the church on Monday, and it might be a cute idea to sell coffee cakes there. There's a little bake sale table and it's always popular. Would you want to do that? Make some coffee cakes for the bazaar? And maybe volunteer at the table for a bit?"

"Sure!" said Kate, who'd rather spend a day baking than do anything else on earth.

Phoebe was very pleased by the notion of combining holiday baking and charity work in one endeavor. It was a very Proper Christmas thing to do. "Definitely," she agreed.

They wrapped up the game — Gee had won, of course — and went upstairs. They were barely out of Gee's earshot when Phoebe grabbed Neeve's arm and dragged her into her room.

Hillary and Kate followed. "So what did you tell the Bradshaws?" she asked desperately.

Neeve smiled. "I said you'd changed your mind. That you'd had a better idea and weren't going to get Gee a dog anymore."

Phoebe's face went white. "You did not!" she said, stating it rather than asking it.

Neeve laughed. "You're right. I didn't. I said that you were coming to look at the dogs on your own, and that if it still seemed like a good idea after you saw them, you were going to bring Gee in on it."

Phoebe didn't love what Neeve had come up with, but at least it had saved her at Coolidge's. "Thanks," she said pensively. "I owe you one."

"Yes, you do, little lady. And don't think I won't remember," said Neeve with a wicked grin.

"I still need to come up with a plan, though," added Phoebe.

"What if we got another adult to vouch for you?" asked Hillary. "Like, what if Sheila told them she'd take responsibility?"

"No," said Phoebe, shaking her head. "We couldn't put her in that position."

"The thing to do," said Kate, surprising them all with her deviousness, "is to get another adult to say they'll take the dog if Gee doesn't want it. You wouldn't even have to tell the Bradshaws beforehand. You could just do the transfer after Christmas if it didn't all work out."

Everyone was silent for a minute, looking for the loophole in the plan. But there wasn't one. It was brilliant! But elation quickly returned to stress as they tried to think of someone.

"My mom would never," said Phoebe.

"It wouldn't be fair to Winnie," said Hillary. "Even though my mom might let me if I play the divorce card really hard." With her parents' divorce nearly final, Hillary's parents felt guilty enough to do almost anything to make her happy.

"My mom just got the living room and family room re-done, and I think she would have a conniption if a puppy came in and trashed everything," said Kate thoughtfully.

"They do make puppy gates," offered Phoebe, ever so helpful.

"If we are truly, truly desperate, I'll ask," said Kate.

"We are," countered Phoebe.

"Hey, what about Farren?" said Neeve suddenly.

There was a surprised silence. Then Phoebe said, "I like it. I really like it!"

Neeve beamed.

"You know," continued Phoebe. "For someone who's so against the idea, you sure are being helpful."

"I guess it's just the Christmas spirit," said Neeve with a laugh.

Gee was at church the next morning (despite Saturday evening mass, she did still go to church on Sundays), and the girls had all arrived in the kitchen to lay their plans for the day. It was worked out with Sheila that they'd all ride in with her to the Bicket Bouquet, the island's large grocery store that was owned by Sloan's — and Sheila's — family, and Phoebe would be dropped off on the way to do her special "Christmas errand." They'd pick her up when they'd finished buying the baking ingredients for all the coffee cakes. The girls had privately decided that they wouldn't contact Farren until Phoebe had talked with the Bradshaws and seen the puppies; there was no use getting everyone worked up until that was all sorted out.

Phoebe, who had stayed up way, way too late reading angel stories, was tired and quiet as she ate her breakfast. She was also nervous and a little irritable. She was starting to think maybe this was all just too complicated and that perhaps she should just forget about the whole idea. She was cranky finishing up her breakfast, and morose as she trudged back upstairs to change. She sat down for a moment to flip through the angel book again, and quickly came across a story in which a Labrador retriever had run to a neighbor's house when its elderly master had fallen down the stairs, and the dog had saved the man's life. Phoebe read the story as a sign: She was meant to read that story, and meant to get a dog from Gee. She'd just have to figure it out from there.

"Oh, oh!" Phoebe fell backward onto her bottom. She'd been crouching on the floor and had tipped back, losing her balance as the puppies climbed all over her, tickling and then scratching with their sharp little nails as they scrabbled for purchase on her skin.

"Are you alright, honey?" Mrs. Bradshaw peered over the gate at Phoebe, but Phoebe was laughing.

"I'm fine. I couldn't be better, actually. They're just so cute!"

Mrs. Bradshaw tucked her pencil behind her ear. She was working at the kitchen table, doing some bookkeeping for the store, while Phoebe played with the dogs in the laundry room off the kitchen. Now Mrs. Bradshaw folded her arms and leaned against the doorway, tilting her head to one side as she considered them.

"I think that one is awfully cute," she said, pointing to the largest of the four remaining puppies.

"They're *all* cute! How could anyone ever pick just one?" said Phoebe. She still hadn't decided how she was going to make it happen, but she just knew that she had to get one of these dogs for Gee. They were the cutest things she'd ever seen. Ever! She picked one up, cupping a hand under its round little belly, which was warm and soft as a cashmere baby blanket.

The dog objected to being lifted though, and he turned his head around and attempted to nip Phoebe playfully with his gentle puppy mouth. Phoebe laughed again and put him down carefully, shooing him off to join his siblings, who were currently destroying an old rawhide chewy toy.

"They're an awful lot of work," said Mrs. Bradshaw. "We're

going to have Maggie fixed after they're all placed. One litter is enough."

"So there were six altogether? And two just left yesterday?"

Mrs. Bradshaw nodded. "And I am pretty sure I've got homes for this one" — she gestured to the only female dog that was left — "and that big guy."

"Don't you want to keep one?" asked Phoebe. She couldn't imagine parting with any.

"Well, John really doesn't. We each have a dog, and a puppy is so much work. And the kids are so busy this year with sports and everything. We just don't have a lot of time. He's trying not to get too attached, but I do think if we ended up with one left, we'd probably keep it." She winked at Phoebe.

"I would. I'd love a puppy," said Phoebe wistfully.

"Have you ever had a dog?" asked Mrs. Bradshaw kindly.

"No. My mom and dad both work a lot, and when they're not working, they really like to focus on us kids. They just say — really, my mom says — it's too much responsibility right now for our family."

Mrs. Bradshaw nodded. "I can certainly agree with that. Although we have such wonderful dogs right now, I can't imagine living without them." She paused, and then asked, "Did your grandmother have a dog before?"

Phoebe blanched, not noticeably, she hoped. She didn't have a guaranteed backup plan in place yet, so she needed to avoid any discussion of Gee and the dog. "Yes. They always had dogs when my dad was growing up. And I know they had at least one golden. She'd love another. Also," Phoebe added responsibly in a stroke of genius, "Gee swims in the sound every day — all year long — and I think it would be safer for her if she had a dog with her. You know?"

Mrs. Bradshaw nodded in agreement. "John told you about our story with Max and the tree, right?"

"Yes. And that's why your sign said 'Guardian Angels,' right?" said Phoebe.

"Exactly." There was a pause, and Mrs. Bradshaw said, "So what do you think?"

"Well, I'm sure she'd love one. I just have to talk to my cousins. . . ."

Mrs. Bradshaw grinned. "Don't forget, they're free! You can't do any better than that for a Christmas present." And then the doorbell rang and Mrs. Bradshaw said, "Oops! I'll just be a moment. That's someone else coming to see the pups."

Phoebe looked at her watch. It was ten twenty-five and they were picking her back up at ten thirty. She sighed and looked over the group of puppies. Of the two that were still available, she liked the littlest one. *The runt of the litter,* she thought. *Just like Wilbur in* Charlotte's Web. *Terrific!* She heard voices coming back down the hall and before she had time to place the new voice, Sloan Bicket came into view. Ugh! Phoebe hadn't seen her since sledding the other day. Leave it to Sloan to taint something even as wholesome and fun as playing with puppies.

"Hello, Phoebe," said Sloan in her usual snotty drawl.

Mrs. Bradshaw looked from one girl to the next. "Oh good,

you know each other. Well, enjoy yourselves. I'll just be in here." And she went back to her work.

"Are you getting a puppy?" said Phoebe, by way of greeting.

"Yes," said Sloan, climbing over the puppy gate to enter the room. She sat down against the dryer and patted the floor next to her to call one of the pups over. "I'm picking one out as my Christmas present. I really wanted a pedigreed dog, like a teacup Chihuahua or something, but my parents said one of these would make a better family dog." She rolled her eyes. "They're so un-chic."

"Oh. Nice," said Phoebe. Typical. Sloan was getting Phoebe's dream Christmas present, and she wasn't even psyched. She didn't deserve one of these dogs.

Phoebe was quickly amused by the fact that none of the dogs would come to Sloan. Of course, they were so busy that they wouldn't come to anyone when they were called, unless that person had food in her hand, but Phoebe wasn't going to tell Sloan that. She just watched Sloan's frustration quickly mount, until Sloan finally reached out and plucked a dog from the fray near the rawhide and swooped him over to sit on her lap. But the dog quickly nipped her hand and she dropped him, flinging him off her lap.

"Ow!" she said, indignantly examining her knuckle. "She broke the skin!"

"He, actually," said Phoebe. "You shouldn't throw them down like that. They can get hurt."

"I didn't *throw* him," said Sloan. "I just set him free."

They were quiet for a second, then Sloan asked Phoebe. "Which one do you like best?"

Phoebe spoke before thinking. "The little one. He's just so curious and funny. And he licked me before. I think he likes me back." She smiled. But then she caught sight of Sloan's face. Her eyes were narrowed and she was sizing up the dogs.

"I think I like him, too," said Sloan.

"Well he's mine!" snapped Phoebe, more forcefully than she'd meant to.

Sloan looked at her disdainfully. "I wasn't saying I was choosing him. Just that I liked him."

"Oh. Sorry," said Phoebe, slightly ashamed.

"Are you taking him home today?" asked Sloan.

"Um, no." Phoebe wasn't sure what to say. "Maybe in a couple of days."

"So he'll go back down to Florida with you?" asked Sloan.

Drat! Why did she have to remember that Phoebe was from Florida? It made Phoebe feel guilty about hating her.

"Um, actually, he's going to stay here at Gee's. He's, uh, our . . . he's our Christmas present to Gee."

Sloan raised one eyebrow. "Wow. That's a nice idea. So she wants a dog?"

"Well, it's a surprise, kind of." Phoebe regretted saying it the second the words were out of her mouth. But she just hadn't been able to think fast enough to lie.

"Oh." Now both of Sloan's eyebrows went all the way up, and she turned to look at the door. She lowered her voice.

"And Mrs. Bradshaw is letting you take him, even though your grandmother might not want him?"

Blast! How did Sloan always know to go for the jugular? "We're still working out the details," said Phoebe, in what she hoped came off as a casual offhanded way.

"I see," said Sloan. Was it Phoebe's imagination or was there an evil tone to Sloan's comment?

Phoebe heard the doorbell ring again, and she looked at her watch. Darn! It was ten thirty-seven, and she'd have to leave. Worse, she'd have to leave Sloan behind with Mrs. Bradshaw and her secret. She could now hear Neeve coming along the passage with Mrs. Bradshaw. (*Poor Mrs. Bradshaw,* Phoebe thought fleetingly. *All this work just to get homes for these puppies!*)

"Don't say anything, okay? To Mrs. Bradshaw?" Phoebe could hear the desperation in her own voice and hoped Sloan couldn't. Like any predator, Sloan liked to take advantage of weakness.

"Obviously," said Sloan, managing to make Phoebe feel like a nitwit for even suggesting such a thing.

And then Neeve was in the doorway, greeting them — even greeting Sloan warmly — and oohing and aahing over the puppies. But they had to go. Gee would be at home and wondering where they were, and Sheila might blab to Gee about where they'd been, and then the secret would be ruined.

So with a promise to call Mrs. Bradshaw with the details the next day, Phoebe left. Mrs. Bradshaw had promised to earmark the runt for Phoebe and Phoebe felt half-grateful, half-guilty for letting her. Leaving Sloan behind was like leaving a lion in a cage full of lambs, but what else could she do? Phoebe took a backward glance as she left, and the innocent look Sloan was giving Mrs. Bradshaw made Phoebe very, very nervous.

CHAPTER FIFTEEN

Angel Cakes

Today was shaping up to be even warmer than yesterday. By the time the Callahan cousins and Sheila returned to The Sound, the sun was high in the sky and the air was nearly balmy. Phoebe was outraged.

"I think it's warmer here than it is in Florida! What happened to all that lovely cold weather you were having up here when I arrived?" she demanded of Sheila, in a mock-mad voice. Phoebe was sitting in the front seat.

"There, there, luv, the winds could change at any time. I don't believe we're in for a warm Christmas. But ya know, the weather's been barmy these past few years. And yer man on the telly is always wrong with his predictions. He says cold and snow, and we get warm and sun. Who knows?"

Phoebe huffed and folded her arms. Neeve had the window down and the warmish air was buffeting everyone in Sheila's wood-paneled Wagoneer. As they crossed the causeway, the water of the sound was indigo and glittered like tinsel in the sun, and thin white clouds were laid high across the sky like brushstrokes, or a sweep of sugar glaze on a Christmas cookie — light and smooth. Sand gathered at the edges of the road where it had collected after the island's four dump trucks had sanded the snowy roads the other day, and the air smelled briny, like a thaw. Phoebe saw people in only sweaters out for a Sunday walk, and rather than enjoying the respite from a cold New England winter along with them, she was mad. *What a rip-off!* she thought. *All this way for a Proper Christmas and look what happens!*

In the kitchen, the girls and Sheila created an assembly line. Hillary and Neeve measured, Phoebe greased the pans, Sheila ran the mixer, and Kate monitored the baking times, which was the most complicated job. Greasing the pans gave Phoebe quite a lot of time off in the beginning, as they only had room to cook cakes in eight of the sixteen pans at a time. So with all sixteen pans greased, she went upstairs and had a look at her Christmas file, just to get an update on how much Proper Christmas stuff they'd accomplished so far. Time was short and Phoebe wanted to make sure they packed it all in.

So: They'd gotten a beautiful tree and decorated it. They'd put out traditional Christmas decorations. They'd done something charitable, and were now doing something else charitable along with the holiday baking. They'd be doing a craft tomorrow night, at the museum sleepover, and caroling was planned. She had a gift idea in mind for Gee, and the others . . . well, the truth was, she would rather just buy something for them. With the homemade gift tags, she rationalized, it would be okay. And then there was the party. That would really be the centerpiece of the Proper Christmas for Phoebe. Their plans reminded her of feasts she'd read about in Edith Wharton novels, or old English country house novels by Rosamund Pilcher or Elizabeth Jane Howard. Elegant, bountiful, gorgeous, but still cozy and festive. Phoebe sighed happily just thinking about all the guests, and the food, and the fancy tablecloths. It would be good.

She still had a few minutes to kill, so she closed the file in satisfaction, and pulled the angel book from her bedside table. One or two angel stories would be pleasurable before lunch.

She took the book to the window seat and sat down comfortably, arranging the pillows behind her back. Then she dove in where she'd left off, among the visitations and communications from beyond that were balm for her very soul. The next story was about an angel on top of a Christmas tree that cried real tears whenever the family members in the house fought. When finally, on Christmas Eve, the family had a big healing talk and truce, the youngest child noticed that the angel was smiling. Phoebe was crying a little as she read it (for Phoebe, crying meant that her eyes welled with tears and she blotted them with her sleeve before they could spill over, but still). Even if the story wasn't true, she wanted to believe it was. The tears were also due to the unfortunate effect of being reminded all over again about breaking Gee's angel. Now she promised herself that when they went to the Christmas Walk in town tonight, she'd look for a suitable replacement to go on top of the tree. Even if it wasn't an angel.

Phoebe rejoined the others in the kitchen just as Lark arrived, and it was time to eat roast chicken sandwiches with potato chips for lunch. Gee had been in and out during the project and was endlessly grateful for what she termed "all of your hard work" although it really wasn't hard, Phoebe thought; not when it was divided among so many willing people. They turned the baked cakes out of their pans and let them cool as they ate their lunch, and after, they slid them into cellophane bags and tied them closed with red and white gingham ribbon, while waiting for the next batch.

Lark had never had the cake before, so they cut up one that had come out ugly but tasty, and she tried it as they worked.

"Wow! Sheila, this is the most delicious coffee cake I've ever had in my whole life!" said Lark, as enthusiastic as ever. "Yum! It's like . . . I don't know. Divine or something."

"It's what angels eat for breakfast," joked Phoebe.

"Yeah, angel cake," added Hillary.

"Hey," said Phoebe. Everyone turned to look at her because something in the tone of her voice sounded serious. "Let's call them that. Right? For a church sale, at Christmas, isn't it wildly appropriate? Angel cakes?" She grinned hopefully. No one was onto her new angel fascination, and she wasn't sure that she was going to clue them in. It was kind of a private thing.

"Yes!" agreed Neeve, first as usual to support a new idea. "We could make little tags shaped like angels!" she added.

"Yeah, and we could write little, like, angel prayers or poems or something on them!" suggested Kate.

"Excellent!"

Phoebe ran to check with Gee, and Gee thought it was an adorable idea. So Phoebe borrowed Gee's little Christmas angel book she'd just bought, and the girls quickly selected a few tidbits to copy. And the rest of the afternoon was spent stenciling, cutting, and neatly printing angel labels that they holepunched and slid onto the cakes' ribbons.

From noon until five they worked, and at the end, they had turned out forty-eight or so angel cakes, give or take a ruined one or two that they just *had* to snack on instead. Kate had also managed to squeeze in a batch of sugar cookies that they'd cut out in the shape of Christmas trees and would decorate tomorrow. By five, they were truly tuckered out. Gee was so impressed by them, she gave everyone a hug, even Sheila, who had quickly turned the project over to the girls after seeing their prowess develop during the first hour of work.

Seeing the cheerful little cakes all lined up neatly with their festive holiday tags and bows made Phoebe inexplicably proud. It was such a humble little labor of love — very *Little House on the Prairie*-ish — and it made her feel all warm and fuzzy; it seemed to be the very essence of Christmas, right there in Gee's kitchen. If she were a hugger like Gee, she would've gone around and given everyone a hug, too. Instead, she wrapped her arms around her chest, almost hugging herself, and beamed.

"Let's hit that Christmas Walk, gang! What do you say?"

Almost everyone agreed that the warm weather contributed to the Christmas Walk's best turnout ever. Crowds surged along Market and Broad Streets, and the Callahans wondered aloud where all these people had been keeping themselves, until they saw the hordes coming from the direction of the ferry dock.

"Aha!" said Phoebe. "Tourists!"

"Wouldn't you come?" asked Neeve. "I mean if you lived on the mainland? It's so cute. It would probably be a tradition; you'd come every year."

When put that way, Phoebe suddenly liked the idea of the tourists. She wished *her* family had a traditional tradition like going to an old-fashioned Christmas walk instead of the weird things they did. She watched the people coming from the dock and tried to keep a friendly smile on her face, as if she were on the Gull Island Welcoming Committee.

The girls strolled from store to store. Both streets were closed to traffic, and there was Christmas music everywhere — spilling out of stores, being sung by carolers in old-fashioned costumes outside Coolidge's, being played on shiny golden trumpets and french horns outside of Summer Reading.

There were little baskets of gingermen and urns of mulled cider or hot chocolate everywhere, and people were happy and smiling and "simply having a wonderful Christmastime," to quote a Christmas song.

The girls ran into Talbot when they stopped by Booker's, and at Mr. Booker's request, he gave each of the girls a new rope bracelet for free. Their old ones had grown sour-smelling and gray and hard by mid-fall, and one by one, they'd all admitted over e-mail that they'd cut them off. Getting new ones was wonderful, and the fact that they were gifts made it even better.

"Cousins forever!" they called in thanks as they departed, their bracelet arms raised in the air.

Next they took a horse-and-carriage ride in the old-timey buggy that came out for local parades and the like. The farmer it belonged to — Mr. Cabot, it turned out, the one whose farm was right by Macaroni Beach — said he had a sleigh, too. But when Phoebe shared her disappointment that they couldn't use it this year, he reassured her that the experience was quite the same. The bells on the horse's harness jingled, and although in this weather, they surely didn't need the lap blanket provided in the back, the girls drew it up over themselves anyway, just for the full experience.

They hopped off at the far end of Broad Street, and made their way back, stopping in to see old friends along the way. Nate Spangleman's flower shop looked as enchanted as ever; it had bowers of pine latticed low across the ceiling, and they gave the near impression of being *inside* a Christmas tree. Nate was overjoyed to see his friends Kate and Hillary again, and he gave all of the girls a sprig of mistletoe to carry with them, in case they ran into a "potential paramour." The girls were all giggling hysterically by the time they left, and were in quite a giddy mood as they climbed the stairs to Edith Munsfield's art studio up the way.

Miss Munsfield had a party going on in her studio, which Kate and Hillary deemed quite unlike her. Uncharacteristically carefree, she welcomed the girls in, gave them glasses of sparkling apple juice and some spiced nuts, and introduced them around to all of her cronies. The art on the walls was all landscapes of Gull now, and Kate drew the girls into a tight knot to explain the brilliance of each painting. Phoebe left enlightened and energized — not the feelings one usually took from a Christmas party, but especially pleasurable for an intellectual like Phoebe in their unexpectedness.

Back on the street, it was getting chillier, which was welcome. The lights on the spokes of the Old Mill twinkled brightly against the black starry sky. Phoebe decided to skip a visit to Summer Reading. She didn't want to see Mr. Bradshaw before she had an iron-clad puppy plan in place. So while Kate and the others popped into the Old Mill, Phoebe went along to the library to see if Mrs. Merrihew might be there.

The library looked just as sweet as the Old Mill. Up close, Phoebe could see how much work must've gone into the holiday decoration of the library, and she was impressed. Libraries weren't usually noted for their stylishness or creativity, so it was doubly impressive to see the work that had gone into this jolly project. In the lobby, a tree was decorated with typical balls and tinsel, and a menorah burned brightly on the circulation desk. People were milling around chatting and drinking something out of paper cups, and nibbling from a cheese log, and it was much noisier than usual. Shockingly noisy, in fact, for a regular library-goer like Phoebe.

Phoebe spotted Mrs. Merrihew across the room all dressed up, with a green paper crown on her head at a jaunty angle. Around her neck was a red and green macaroni necklace. Phoebe smiled and made her way through the crowd to say hello. Shy as she was about saying hello, she wanted to see if they had any books on the whaling era; she wanted to do a little research of her own before the sleepover tomorrow, just to enrich the experience.

She arrived at Mrs. Merrihew's side, prompting a big hug from Mrs. Merrihew, and introductions all around to the friends she was chatting with. She billed Phoebe as a "voracious reader and researcher, maybe even a future librarian," while Phoebe smiled shyly and graciously accepted the compliments. The other people drifted away and Phoebe and Mrs. Merrihew had a little catch-up chat. Then Phoebe told her about the sleepover at the museum, about all the cousins going, and Lark joining them, and everything, and she explained what she was looking for.

Mrs. Merrihew clapped her hands, slightly dislodging her

holiday crown (made by her grandson, as it turned out, along with the necklace), and, seizing Phoebe enthusiastically by the arm, propelled her across the room to a groaning wall of local history books, where she deposited her with an uncharacteristically airy wave at the second shelf.

Mrs. Merrihew then flitted back to the growing crowd, the hostess of the library, like a queen in her castle. Phoebe laughed after her. Mrs. Merrihew was never usually like this; the Christmas spirit (*or spirits,* Phoebe thought wryly) must've taken hold of her.

Phoebe dragged a rolling stepstool over to the shelf and sat down, removing her jacket and folding it across her lap. She bent her head to read the titles sideways, pulling potentially interesting books out and flipping through them. There was a lot of information about the whaling trade in other, similar places, like Sag Harbor, New York, and Nantucket, Massachusetts, but very little about Gull.

So Phoebe contented herself with glancing at accounts of voyage supply lists, and daily logs, and crew rosters. But the last book she found had some of the information she was seeking. It mentioned Gull Island frequently, talked about trade, and the things that whalers — particularly captains — brought home for their families, and listed the things they liked to buy, and eat, and how they decorated their houses. There was bound to be some holiday information in the book somewhere, and in addition to having run out of time in her search (she had to go find the others), Phoebe despaired of finding anything more specific than this. So she snapped the book shut decisively, checked it out at the desk, and went to say goodbye to Mrs. Merrihew before she left to rejoin the others outside the Fudge Company, as planned.

It didn't take more than a second to spot the green crown from across the room. But just as she and Mrs. Merrihew made eye contact, Phoebe realized with a jolt that Mrs. Merrihew was standing with the Bickets. Including Sloan. Phoebe stopped in her tracks and tried to get off with a wave, but Mrs. Merrihew beckoned her over enthusiastically, and Phoebe had to go.

"Hi," she said to Sloan. "Hello, Mr. and Mrs. Bicket," she added. They exchanged pleasantries and then, of course, Mrs. Merrihew asked Phoebe if she'd found what she was looking for. Relieved that she would get off easily, Phoebe agreed that yes, she had, and she began saying her thank yous and goodbyes, edging away from the little group before Mrs. Merrihew could say more about why Phoebe was there.

But it wasn't to be. Mrs. Merrihew launched into "Phoebe's big adventure" and described it to the Bickets, even going so far as to prod Phoebe about the name of her "cute little friend" who was going with them. By the time she'd finished, Phoebe was red with mortification and Sloan looked both amused and hurt. Her parents looked as clueless as Mrs. Merrihew, and knowing how Sloan never let on any sign of weakness to her parents, Phoebe guessed she probably wouldn't tell them that she was hurt by the exclusion. Phoebe was relieved *and* doubly mortified by this realization. On the whole, it was a ghastly interaction, and Phoebe didn't know what to say or do. So she'd said a hasty goodbye and fled the library, vowing never to return when there was a party there again.

She quickly backtracked up Broad Street, then crossed to where she could see the cousins standing outside the Fudge Company. Clutching her book in her arm, she drew nearer and saw that they were all eating candy canes jammed in lemon halves. It was a bizarre pairing and momentarily distracted her from the rant she was about to begin.

"What are those?" she asked, her nose wrinkling in distaste.

"I know, they look weird . . . ," began Hillary.

"But they're delicious!" finished Kate.

"You start sucking on the top of the candy cane, and somehow the acid from the lemon burns a hole up the candy cane. Then, when you suck more, the lemon juice comes up only it's been sweetened by the candy cane on the way up, so it tastes like minted lemonade. Want me to go get you one?" Neeve was clearly revved by the sugar.

Phoebe waved a hand at her dismissively. "No, thanks. Listen, you guys, something really bad just happened . . . ," and she described in detail the scene at the library. At the end, she dropped her head into her hands and shook it from side to side.

"Oh dear," said Kate sympathetically.

"Well . . . ," began Hillary.

"We have to invite her now," said Neeve decisively.

"Oh, come on, Neeve," protested Phoebe. She had known someone would say that. "We have to ruin the whole night just because of Mrs. Merrihew's indiscretion?"

Phoebe saw Kate look at Hillary for a translation. She sighed heavily and provided it herself. "Slip of the lips? Blurting?" She added, until she saw comprehension dawn in Kate's eyes.

Kate then looked at Neeve. "I agree with Neeve. We have to at least ask her."

Hillary was nodding. *Oh! This can't be happening!* thought Phoebe.

"Actually," said Hillary rationally. "I think Phoebe has to ask her."

"Ack!" said Phoebe. But she knew they were right. "You mean, if I see her again tonight, or I can call her tomorrow?" Somehow, putting it off made it seem a tad easier. And maybe if she waited until tomorrow, Sloan would already have plans. In fact, Phoebe was sure she already did.

"I think tonight," said Kate sadly. She knew Phoebe was bummed.

"Yes. Either find her or call her." Neeve was firm and Phoebe's heart sunk.

"Oh, fine. Just fine."

CHAPTER SIXTEEN

Angel Pins

They didn't run into Sloan again until they were on their way to meet Gee, who had gone to get the car from up by Cabot's and swing around to the memorial on Fisher's Path and scoop up the girls.

Despite the Sloan invitation hanging over her head, Phoebe's mood was buoyed by her purchase of an enormous golden papier-mâché star from a Christmas crafts stand in the park by the police station. It was for the top of Gee's tree and it was enchanting, like a star that a fairy would make — all squiggly rays and little balls on the end of each point. It was big and happy and cute and Phoebe couldn't wait to go home and put it on the tree. And just as she was truly gloating about the purchase, out stepped Sloan, from a dessert tasting at Callie's Cupboard. All alone, she looked just as surprised to run into the Callahans as they were to run into her.

Phoebe was dumbstruck, but the other girls quickly recovered and gave Sloan warm, if slightly muted, greetings; it was almost as if they were apologizing for not having invited her earlier to the sleepover. Clutching the star like a shield, Phoebe began to sputter. Finally she got the words out.

"Um, Sloan, ah, you know, we were talking, and we thought . . . ah . . . that it would be nice if you could join us tomorrow night. Um, at the museum sleepover." There, she'd said it! She closed her mouth and stared at Sloan, waiting for a reply.

Sloan hesitated for just a fraction of a second, and then she said breezily, "No thanks. I can't. I have a date." And she brushed past them and continued on up the street.

Phoebe pursed her lips and blew out a stream of air, half in relief and half in annoyance that Sloan had once again had the last word. "All's well that ends well," she said, and she turned to the others.

Kate looked pained, as if she felt terribly guilty, and Neeve was pensive. Hillary didn't look anything. She wasn't into girly-girl drama, so she just took everything at face value. She probably believed Sloan that she had a date tomorrow night, and didn't think anything even of *that*. Phoebe had to laugh. She elbowed Hillary and said, "C'mon. Let's go."

Although bewildered by the elbow, Hillary followed her, and then so did Kate and Neeve, Kate taking one last look over her shoulder at Sloan walking alone into the crowd.

After dinner that night, everyone watched *It's a Wonderful Life.* Even Sheila, who Phoebe thought she might have seen crying. (Phoebe always had to check to see who cried at the sad parts in movies, and it really annoyed her mother and her older sister when she did it to them. They were big ones for weeping in films.)

Up in bed, Phoebe was reading a new angel book with her Itty Bitty Book Light so as not to disturb Hillary, who was trying to go to sleep. Suddenly, Phoebe heard Hillary giggling in her bed.

"What?" asked Phoebe with a smile, willing to share a joke as she marked her page with a finger.

"I just got it. Why you elbowed me after we saw Sloan. She's not really going on a date, is she?"

"I think not," said Phoebe with a smile. But it was a rueful smile, because she actually felt pretty bad about the whole thing after all.

The next morning they were all dressed and downstairs by eight. The Christmas bazaar started at nine, and they had to get there to help set up. The plan was for them to lay out all the baked goods for the bake sale table, then stay on as volunteers to mind the table until ten, when they'd be free. Then they had to be at the museum by three for the sleepover, so Phoebe had the middle of the day to get to Farren and figure out the puppy thing. She was desperate to get it organized because she wanted to be able to get back to Mrs. Bradshaw today.

The girls were excited to be out the door so early, and they were looking forward to being useful at the bazaar. They'd all dressed festively — Phoebe had on a red turtleneck and little ornament dangly earrings, and Kate was wearing a wrap-around felt skirt. When they went outside to get in the Volvo, Phoebe was thrilled because, just as Sheila had predicted, a cold wind had arrived overnight, and a frost had set in, so it felt Christmassy again. Gee chauffeured them and the cakes to the church — making an out-of-the-way stop in town to get cinnamon donuts and orange juice at the News Co. for a quick breakfast in the car.

They arrived at the church amidst much bustle and activity. Cars and vans were being unloaded in the parking lot by local residents and visiting craftspeople and vendors alike. In the basement, there were long tables set up, and just inside the door, a big pile from a tablecloth rental place on the mainland — all red and green tablecloths for people to pick up and use on their tables. Mrs. Hagan, who ran the sailing clinic the girls attended in the summer, was there with a clipboard, organizing everyone. She greeted the girls warmly, handed them a cash box that already contained some change, and directed them to their table (Phoebe had almost blurted out that Mrs. Hagan looked so different without the zinc oxide on her lower lip that she didn't recognize her, but she decided not to say it at the last moment). Kate selected a red tablecloth for their table because it would go nicely with the ribbons on the angel cakes, and then they all headed over to table four, where Mrs. Hagan had directed them.

Phoebe and Kate spread out the cloth, which pooled prettily at the floor, hiding the metal table legs. They lined up all the angel cakes, tweaking the bows to make them look as cute as possible, and arranging the angel tags so they laid just so. Then they began receiving cartons and boxes of other donated baked goods from people, plus platters and pans full of things, and all sorts of treats to arrange. Kate took charge of that, laying everything out attractively, and putting the overstock under the table where they could reach it to restock when things started to run low.

Then suddenly it was nine and the doors opened and a stream of shoppers wandered in. Before the girls knew it, they'd sold six angel cakes, and then twelve total, and there was a buzz around the hall about them. People kept coming over to buy them and exclaim over how cute they were, with the ribbons and tags and all, and Phoebe was very pleased. The din in the hall rose to a clamor, and Christmas music was playing on someone's boom box, and the table selling decorative candles was burning all sorts of fragrant incenses and candles, the smell of which mingled with coffee and cider from urns by the volunteers' station, and cinnamon from the bake sale table, right under Phoebe's nose. Their hour of work flew by, and they'd sold twenty cakes, and they were just filling in the new volunteers who'd arrived to take over, when along came Sloan.

"So what's good?" asked Sloan by way of greeting.

"Um," Phoebe felt a little shy about pushing their own product, but what the heck. "I can only vouch for the angel cakes, because we made them. They're sour cream coffee cakes and they're delicious."

"Sheila's recipe?" asked Sloan, looking Phoebe directly in the eye.

Phoebe nodded.

"It's my father's family recipe. My grandma used to make them all the time. Been there, eaten that. And what did you call them? Something about angels?" Sloan tilted her head in a kind of mock-confusion, as though to imply that Phoebe and the others were being presumptuous by giving a new name to Sloan's family recipe.

"Yes." Phoebe was turned off by Sloan's rudeness, as usual. She stood up as straight as possible and looked Sloan in the eye. "Angel cakes."

"Oh my God," said Sloan in a condescending voice. "Angels are so over."

Phoebe would have thought the same thing only days ago, but now she was indignant. "Over? How can angels be *over*? They can't *go* anywhere. They're everywhere, and they're here to stay."

With an incredulous smile on her face, Sloan mimed looking around and then over her shoulder. Then she leaned into Phoebe and said sarcastically, "Where?"

Phoebe huffed in annoyance. "Whatever," she said.

"Yeah. *Exactly,*" agreed Sloan. "Whatever."

"So do you want anything or not, because our shift is over." Kate and Neeve were already shopping around at some of the other tables, and Hillary was standing to the side of the bake sale table, chatting with one of the other volunteers while she waited for Phoebe.

"I think I'll just take a bag of this homemade granola," said Sloan.

"Knock yourself out," muttered Phoebe, as she took Sloan's money and made change.

"Thanks. Have fun at your sleepover," said Sloan as she left. Somehow, her tone of voice managed to insinuate that sleep-overs were the lamest thing going, and Phoebe was even more irked than before.

"Yeah. Right," sputtered Phoebe. "And you, too, on your date!" she called after Sloan, but it didn't look like Sloan had heard her, or at least she didn't turn back around.

"*Blast!*" Phoebe growled in frustration. "Come on, Hillary. Let's go."

Hillary quickly said her goodbyes to their replacements and scrambled to catch up with Phoebe, who was now stalking away in the opposite direction from where Sloan went. Phoebe was furious and felt triply insulted as she relayed the conversation to Hillary. First, that Sloan was bored by their cake recipe, second, the angel comment, and third, the thing about the sleepover.

"Hey, hey, hey! Calm down, girl!" said Hillary. "Listen, she's just jealous. Don't let it get to you."

"Why does she always have to be such a jerk?" stormed Phoebe. *And why do I always let her get the better of me?* she thought angrily.

"Just don't let her bother you. If you do, then she wins, and it's score one for Sloan." Hillary always spoke in sports analogies when emotions ran high. Phoebe had to smile at it, and smiling made her feel slightly better.

Neeve and Kate were stopped up ahead by a table that was very busy with customers, and Phoebe headed toward them. But just before she reached the cousins, another table caught her eye. It was a whole table of angels and angel stuff! Phoebe couldn't believe it! She stopped, but Hillary kept on going, focused on what the others had found; she didn't give Phoebe a second glance, almost as if she hadn't noticed her stopping. Phoebe shrugged. She'd catch up to them in a minute.

She greeted the pretty, heavyset woman behind the table, and then she looked up and down the table's length. She didn't even know where to begin. There were angel books, tapes of "angel music," angel ornaments, candles to burn to attract certain kinds of angels, angel jewelry, mugs with angels on them. Most of it was pretty junky, like the stuff at the mall back home. But about ten percent of it was traditional and beautiful, and that was what appealed to Phoebe. The bottom line was, she didn't particularly like masses of angels, or angels as decorative motifs (save for holiday decorations), but she did like the plain and simple religious stuff that felt like it might actually work.

Phoebe saw the cousins moving on to a table of beads that was farther along the hall, but Phoebe stayed put for another few minutes. She sorted through small, leather-bound prayer books, looked at a little kit for making an altar to pray at, examined a slender, pretty vial of holy water, and then she came upon the guardian angel pins. They were cherubs, gold and miniature — no bigger than half an inch, and they had a little post sticking out of their backs, like an earring, with a backing to keep them in place. Each one was pinned to a colorfully decorated index card–sized piece of heavy paper, and each card had a different little prayer or bit of angel scripture from the Bible on it. They were five dollars each. Quickly, Phoebe made her decision, gathering up six of them (one each for herself, the cousins, and Sheila and Gee) and paying the lady behind the table. Then she took the brown paper bag from the lady, wished her a merry Christmas, and caught up with the others.

But now, with her own shopping complete, Phoebe got antsy. She needed to get home and call Farren and start figuring out the dog problem. By the time everyone else had finished shopping, it was eleven thirty, and then they needed to call Gee or Sheila from the pay phone to come get them, and then they had to wait for them to arrive. Phoebe craned her neck as they drove past the Little Store. Farren's car was parked out front, and Phoebe felt a flash of nerves and excitement as they passed.

CHAPTER SEVENTEEN

Calls

$\mathcal{I}$t was twelve fifteen when they got home, and Sheila was there in the kitchen.

"Phoebe, luv, there was a call for you." Sheila squinted at a small piece of paper. "Sally called and asked that you ring her back."

Sally? Phoebe stared at Sheila blankly, racking her brain.

"Said it was about the gift? Fer yer grandmother?"

Oh! Sally! Sally was Mrs. Bradshaw! The fog cleared from Phoebe's brain.

"Okay. Thanks, Sheila. I'll just run upstairs and use the phone there."

Darn! Phoebe wished she'd had the Farren thing all organized and had been able to call Mrs. Bradshaw first! She dashed up to the phone. She was so nervous, she was shaking as she dialed the number for the Little Store, and as the phone rang once, twice, three times, she started to dread that

Farren might have just left. But finally, on the fourth ring, Farren picked up, slightly breathless.

"Hi, Farren, it's Phoebe Callahan," Phoebe said quickly.

"Phoebe! *Shalom! Aloha!* How are you? I'd heard you were back!"

Phoebe had to grin at Farren's nontraditional greeting, and then everything quickly became easier. They caught up a little on news, and then Phoebe cleared her throat and her nervousness returned.

"So, Farren, um, I was calling because, well, it's a secret, for starters, so please don't say anything to Gee. But, we want to get her a puppy, from the Bradshaw's litter, for Christmas? And . . ."

"Oh! What a wonderful idea! It's very good karma to give live presents, you know. Great choice. . . ."

Phoebe had to interrupt her, or Farren might go off on one of her kooky tangents. "Right. Thanks. So, the thing is, we want it to be a surprise . . ."

"Poor Mrs. Callahan. You girls are going to kill her one of these days with all of your secrets and surprises. I'm telling you, it's not healthy. Make sure she's getting enough Omega-3 for her heart. Tell her I said so. And wheat germ. . . ."

"Okay, but anyway, we need to be able to tell the Bradshaws that if we take one of the puppies, and Gee doesn't want him, well . . . that he has a home. Like, so we guarantee that we're going to keep him, or that someone nice will, if Gee doesn't want him. See?" Phoebe hadn't directly asked, but she was hoping Farren got her drift.

"I see."

"You do?" Phoebe was elated.

"Yes. So who can we think of who might want a puppy?" mused Farren.

Oh. "Well, we were hoping, maybe you?" Phoebe asked tentatively.

"Me?!" Farren was shocked by the idea. Phoebe could hear it over the phone even. *Blast!*

"Yes. Wouldn't you love a golden retriever puppy? I just was there playing with them yesterday. They are so cute, just adorable. And I think you could really use a dog. You're there all day alone in the store, more or less. . . ."

"Wait, wait, slow down. A dog. That is a heavy idea, man. Heavy. I don't know if I really want to be responsible for something, someone, else in my life right now. Hmm. And none of you can take a dog home?"

"No, for a variety of reasons," said Phoebe.

Farren was quiet on the other end. "You know, a dog isn't something you just rush into."

"I know," agreed Phoebe.

"Do you think your grandmother actually wants a dog?" asked Farren. Sometimes Farren was like this; she snapped out of her whole "groovy" thing and acted like a real adult for a few minutes.

"I think so. Anyway, you said it's good karma."

"For you, Phoebe. For the giver. Receiving an unwanted creature is a whole other story. It can really mess up your aura and play with your energy in funny ways."

"Well, what do you say? Will you be our backup?" pressed Phoebe, feeling desperate again, now that she sensed she was losing Farren's moment of clarity and maybe with it her best shot at getting Farren to say yes.

"Hmm. I need to meditate on it. When do you need to know by?"

Phoebe paused. "Like in half an hour?" she suggested tentatively.

"Half an hour! Holy guacamole!"

Phoebe smiled. "So?" she pressed.

"I'll call you back," said Farren. And she hung up.

Phoebe hung up, too, and she drummed her fingers on the table. Should she call Mrs. Bradshaw back now? Or should she wait until Farren called her? It would kind of be a waste of a call if she did it now, since she had no new information. On the other hand, putting it off would just make her nervous. From her work as an editor of the school paper back home, she knew it was best to make dreaded phone calls as quickly as possible or your dread would grow, the longer you put them off.

Taking a deep breath for courage, Phoebe dialed the Bradshaw's number.

When Mrs. Bradshaw answered, Phoebe identified herself

and explained that they'd been out working at the Christmas bazaar or she'd have called back sooner.

"That's okay, honey. I was just touching base because we're down to the last pup — that cute little runt you liked — and I have someone interested in him. Actually, it's the young lady who was here when you were here the other day. Sloan Bicket. She'd like him for Christmas, but I said you'd already staked your claim. I just needed to know where things stand for you." She paused politely for Phoebe to answer, but Phoebe was speechless. Her heart had sunk like lead as soon as she'd heard Sloan's name, and she hadn't really heard much else after that.

Sloan Bicket wanted her dog. Well, Gee's dog. Her brilliant present idea for Gee. The nerve! Sloan knew that was the dog that Phoebe wanted. How could she just go after him like that? She was evil. No matter what the other cousins said about Sloan's flashes of niceness or that she was good when she was alone, Phoebe knew she was truly evil.

"Hello?" Mrs. Bradshaw seemed to be wondering if Phoebe had hung up.

"I'm here," said Phoebe. "Uh, yes, we're going to take him," she blurted. Then she bit her lip. How could she? What if Farren said no and Gee said no and she was stuck with a puppy she couldn't have? Then what? *Well, then I'll have to cross that bridge when I come to it,* she told herself firmly. *Just so long as Sloan doesn't get her hands on him.*

"Great!" said Mrs. Bradshaw. "I'm sure he'll be very happy with your grandmother."

"I agree." Phoebe cringed; she hated being dishonest. "But, just don't say anything to my grandmother, okay? It's going to be a surprise from all of us kids."

"Okay. But you're sure she wants him, aren't you, sweetie?"

Phoebe paused. This had been what she was dreading. "Uh . . . ," she stalled. "Well, if for any reason it doesn't work out, which is highly unlikely, ah, my cousin is going to take him." There. She hadn't totally lied. One of her cousins might take him. She just didn't know which one yet. But Mrs. Bradshaw seemed to be okay with that.

"Alright. So when do you want to come get him? Or should we bring him to you?"

Phew!, Phoebe thought in relief. "I think . . . um . . ." They could probably keep him up in Sheila's room on Christmas eve. Gee wouldn't hear him up there.

They worked out a plan for him to be dropped off on Christmas Eve at eight o'clock, and Phoebe would meet her at the bottom of the driveway so Gee didn't notice the headlights. Mrs. Bradshaw offered to bring some of his food and some treats, just to get them through to the twenty-sixth when the stores opened up again, and Phoebe was grateful. Mrs. Bradshaw declined any offer of money and Phoebe made a mental note to drop a little gift off for her at the bookstore. Then they said their goodbyes, with Phoebe thanking Mrs. Bradshaw profusely.

At the very end, Mrs. Bradshaw said, "Oh, Phoebe, I'm so glad it's you taking him home and not Sloan. I know I shouldn't say this but I just didn't feel good about him going home with her. She seems like somewhat of an unhappy girl."

"She is," Phoebe said grimly. And they hung up.

Downstairs again, Phoebe grabbed the cousins and waved them up to her shared room for a conference. Everyone was looking at her with curiosity, but she didn't say anything until they were all safely in and the door was pulled closed behind them.

"Okay. We've got the dog for Gee," she announced.

"Yippee!" squealed Kate. "I knew Farren would say yes!"

"Um, that's the one thing." Phoebe frowned. "She didn't."

No one said anything for a minute while they digested this news. "You mean she said no?" said Hillary finally.

"No. She's calling me back. But in the meantime, I had to call Mrs. Bradshaw back, and I wound up just telling her that we'd worked it all out and the answer was yes."

"But why?" Neeve shook her head in confusion.

"Well, because . . . ," Phoebe dreaded telling the others about Sloan, but she knew she had to come clean. "Because there was only one dog left and Sloan wanted him and I saw how she was with the dogs the other day and I swear it's not because I hate her, although it's partially that, but mostly because I just don't think she deserves him and she really wants a teacup *Chihuahua,* and I just really *want* this dog. I mean, I want *Gee* to have him." Phoebe was embarrassed by her misspeaking. She held her breath as she waited for Neeve or Hillary to call her on it (Kate never would), but no one said anything at all.

After about thirty seconds, Neeve spoke. "Then it's settled. It's a great present and if Gee doesn't want him, we'll just take it from there."

Phoebe couldn't believe her ears. "Really? You mean you're copacetic with it?"

"I have no idea what that word means, but if it means fine then yes. It's done. What else can we do?"

Phoebe nearly hugged Neeve, she was so grateful. "Thanks, Neeve," she said warmly. She loved that Neeve always dealt with problems so well; she just moved on to the solution and never dwelled on things that couldn't be changed. Like Gee, Phoebe realized.

"Bold move, Bee," said Hillary, with a note of admiration in her voice.

"Thanks, I think," grinned Phoebe. Maybe it would all work out after all. "Now let's pack."

CHAPTER EIGHTEEN

Sleepwalking

$\mathscr{P}$hoebe was lying on her bed reading about whaling, waiting for it to be two forty-five or for Farren to call back. She was all packed and ready to go, and everyone else was still struggling to get their things together.

Whaling history made interesting reading, and she felt that she had a pretty good grasp of the industry, now, and what Gull must've been like back in those days.

"Girls! Time to go!" Gee called up the stairs.

Blast! Farren hadn't called back. Phoebe picked up her summer tote bag, filled with her gear, and grabbed the sleeping bag Sheila had rustled up for her, and she went to stand by the door. Hillary was having a hard time cramming her sleeping bag into its little carrier, so Phoebe waited until she was ready and they went down together.

Gee was in the front hall with another huge tote at her feet.

She gestured to it. "Dinner, breakfast and snacks, courtesy of Sheila Bicket," she said with a smile.

Phoebe winced at the reminder of Sheila's last name, but she was looking forward to finding out what Sheila had packed. She grabbed the tote from Gee went out the front door and over to Gee's car to stow the things. Hillary followed and Neeve and Kate appeared seconds later. Phoebe opened the car door, but just then, Sheila appeared at the front door to the house, calling her name.

"Phone call, luv! Says its important!" Phoebe's heart leapt. It had to be Farren. She raced back inside and picked up the extension in the living room.

"Hello?" she said hopefully.

"Hey, baby." It was Farren. "Listen, I've been doing some deep thinking on this and, I have to say, I am just not in the right place right now for a dog. I am so sorry, honey. I'd love to help you out in case things don't work out, but it wouldn't be fair to the little guy. I'm just . . . not responsible enough right now and I've got all I can handle with the store and every-thing. Listen, though, I can try to help you find someone else, okay?"

"Oh." Phoebe didn't know what else to say. "Okay, then. Thanks anyway."

They said their goodbyes and Phoebe hung up the phone and walked slowly back to the car.

"Everything okay, sweetheart?" Gee asked from the front seat.

"Yup." Phoebe tried to put on a happy face; there was no need to worry Gee — not when she couldn't even explain what the problem was.

And then they were off, first to pick up Lark and then to the museum.

"And this was the dining room," Jessie was saying. "All of their meals would have been served here by servants, for when the whaling industry was doing well here, in the 1840s and 1850s, a captain would have been very prosperous indeed. For Christmas dinner, they would have had turkey or ham, mince pie, potatoes or sweet potatoes, and for dessert, plum pudding. Oranges would also have been a very traditional treat around Christmastime. They were hard to get ahold of, and involved well-timed trade with the tropics and careful handling so they didn't spoil in transit."

Phoebe smiled at the idea. Oranges were practically a dime a dozen back home. She looked around the room, which was set up as if for a Christmas dinner. There were pretty pewter serving plates, and fine china and crystal. Red ribbons were tied to the back of each person's chair, and a Christmas stocking hung from each one, bulging with little gifts and treats. Holly was laid along the table and a red runner ran the length of the white tablecloth, cross-stitched (probably by family members) with a decorative Christmas motif. Phoebe would've loved living back then. Furniture and decoration were simple and plain, clothes were handmade and sturdy and modest, and pastimes besides work were wholesome and serious, like reading and furniture making. She could've been very happy . . .

Jessie interrupted Phoebe's thoughts. "And speaking of oranges, they'll be the centerpiece of our traditional craft in a little bit. We're going to make old-fashioned pomanders."

"Oh, nice!" said Phoebe admiringly.

"What's a pomander?" asked Hillary.

Jessie explained. "They're little Christmas-scented sachets that you can put in a bowl or a drawer or hang somewhere special. You take an orange, and a big pile of whole cloves, and you push the cloves into the orange in rows, or in a pretty pattern, however you like. They smell wonderful." She smiled and Phoebe smiled back.

Phoebe was in her element. She loved, loved, loved to learn things — especially historical things. Especially because it made her feel connected to the past, or like she was keeping people's memories alive for them. And she was enjoying herself today because their tour guide and chaperone, Jessica, or Jessie as she called herself, was fun, nice, and smart.

A small, wiry girl with horn-rimmed granny glasses, pale freckly skin, and short, curly red hair, Jessie was in her mid-twenties. When the museum director had greeted them earlier and introduced them to Jessica, she said Jessica was getting her doctorate, so she had to be smart, Phoebe figured. But most importantly, she was one of those people who could make history come alive just by talking about it.

Phoebe could perfectly picture the Hand family living here. Jessie had showed them photos of John, the father, Harriet, the mother, and the three children: Walter, Daniel, and Virginia. Much of their furniture remained in the house (or anyway, the museum had bought stuff that would have been there when they were there), and with the traditional Christmas decorations and fake presents all around the parlor, it looked as if they could walk in at any moment.

Phoebe was really enjoying herself. *It would be fun to work here one day, just like Jessie,* she thought.

They'd spent a lot of time in the "back parlor," which had been converted into a room dedicated to an exhibit about the technicalities of whaling. They'd learned about the different kinds of whale and what they were sought after for (Jessie was impressed that Phoebe already knew from her own research that sperm whales provided oil for candles and sometimes very valuable ambergris that was a perfume base, while baleen from other whales was used for making corsets and hoop skirts when fashion dictated it). They learned all about the different kinds of boats that were used, and studied a graphic painting of a chase. Jessie read them a gory scene from Moby Dick about a whale chase that was so dramatic the hair on the back of Phoebe's neck stood up, even though she'd read the book herself already. Lark was particularly intrigued by whale populations and where they were found, since her parents were marine biologists and she lived and breathed their work. Jessie told them everything she knew about it.

It was really cool to have the museum all to themselves. The girls were allowed to touch anything they wanted, and they could go inside the exhibit rooms, simply lifting the velvet ropes and crossing into the contained little worlds that were preserved there. They could sit on the floor anywhere they wanted and just listen to Jessie's stories, and they could talk as loudly as they wanted. Phoebe was reminded over and over again of things from the Frankweiler book; she felt like Claudia, the main character, when she was wandering through the Metropolitan Museum of Art, deciding where she'd sleep that night.

Their tour lasted about an hour and a half, and then it was time to do the craft. They went back to the kitchen (Jessie explained that a cooking kitchen would've stood outside the house in the backyard to keep fire and heat and smoke away from the house, but that this space would've been used for some food preparation and storage, too), and found the supplies for the craft all laid out on the table. Jessie showed them what their finished product could look like, and how they should push in the cloves, and then they were off and running. She turned on her iPod to play a mix she'd made for them of sea shanties, and old-fashioned American Christmas carols, and they whipped their way through two or three pomanders each.

By six o'clock, they were restless with the activity, so they gathered up all the picnic things and set out their meal. Sheila had packed baked ham sliced paper-thin, with cheddar biscuits to make little sandwiches and honey mustard sauce. There was cheese and crackers with savory onion jam, and fruit, and a salad that they could add dressing to and then shake in its big, lidded container to toss. For dessert, she'd made little date puddings with heavy caramel sauce to pour over the top. Phoebe was especially impressed by Sheila's effort to be somewhat historical in her food choices, whereas everyone else was just happy it was delicious.

While they ate, Phoebe looked around happily at everyone else. She was so glad Sloan hadn't come, after all. She would have just ruined it. Phoebe knew it wasn't charitable of her to think such a thing at Christmastime, but it was true.

After dinner, they changed into their pj's and Jessie ran the educational movie for them in the little auditorium in the basement. They ate popcorn, which Jessie explained would've been a traditional treat for children in that era, and afterward, Jessie ran a little trivia game to see how much information they'd already picked up. Naturally, Phoebe won.

By nine o'clock, the girls were getting tired. Phoebe was really feeling that the past had been better than the present until Jessie showed them where the outhouse was. She teased them for a few minutes that they'd have to go out in the cold to use it or find a chamber pot instead, and Phoebe quickly readjusted her thinking about the past. Obviously, there *had* been some improvements in the world over time. Everyone used the public bathroom to get ready for bed, which was funny and just how Phoebe had imagined the kids in the Frankweiler book doing it. Neeve wet her hair when she was washing her face, but she used the hand dryer to dry it afterward, which Lark found a scream. And then it was time for the goodnight story.

They were sleeping in the front bedroom that had belonged to fourteen-year-old Virginia Hand. It had a big canopied bed and a fireplace, plus a little writing desk and a clothes press. Instead of wooden slats, the bed was made of wood lashed together with rope — almost like a hammock with a frame — and the mattress was horsehair. It looked lumpy and kind of dirty, so the girls all opted to sleep on the plank floor with its rag rug, even Phoebe. Jessie had a little camp cot set up for herself in the master bedroom across the hall.

Everyone settled down into their sleeping bags — Phoebe had her bumblebee beanbag with her for coziness, and she noticed that Hillary had a scrap of her old baby blanket, Pinky. Then Jessie turned out all the lights upstairs except for a little fake oil lantern she had, and she began her story.

"Now, this is a true story from the days of the Hand family. We've pieced it together with local records and family archives, as well as a log that survives from Captain Hand's vessel, the *Starbuck*. I'm going to tell you three-quarters of it tonight, and then I'll tell you the rest in the morning, after you've had a chance to see if you can guess what the ending is.

"Early in the morning of December 21, 1843, the Hand household was all abuzz with activity. It was still dark outside, but all the leaded glass windows were ablaze with lanterns that burned with sperm oil and lit up the rooms like daylight. You see, the *Starbuck* was setting sail that day, and Mrs. Hand, Harriet, had finally convinced her husband to take his family along with him. As you know, whaling captains were separated for long periods of time from their families when they were out at sea — sometimes years — and it was very hard on the wives and children that they left behind. No matter how much money they'd earned to keep their families nicely while they were away, American society back then was not kind to women on their own, and it could even be dangerous for a woman to be negotiating her way through months and years without a man to protect her and her interests.

"Ships that carried women to sea were known as 'hen frigates,' a pejorative term that conveyed sailors' feelings about having women onboard. For while some women could be as useful as men at sea, there wasn't anything they added. Ships *had* men who could cook, men who could sew, and men who could nurse. Women were a distraction and simply a reminder of what the men had all left behind.

"So, that cold December morning, the Hand household was packed and ready. The children had lesson plans from their masters to learn at sea; there were special medicines carefully stored in cotton batting, and some special foods for the children, so they didn't get any of the diseases of malnourishment that sailors often got, like scurvy and rickets. Harriet Hand was probably very excited and absolutely terrified. Her mother had spent the night at the house, along with her younger sister, and I'm certain that they expected they'd never see Harriet again. Whaling voyages were long and dangerous, and anything could happen to either the people at sea or the ones who were waiting at home for them over those many months and years. You can just imagine the scene as Harriet goes anxiously from room to room, making sure the children are dressed and ready, making sure every stitch of luggage has been taken down to the wagon to be carried in loads to the dock. Just imagine yourself packing for your Christmas trip to Gull and multiply it by a hundred."

Here Jessie paused to take a gulp of the tea she had in an insulated mug next to her. Phoebe was enraptured by the story. "Don't stop!" she cried, her eyes shining in the lamplight.

"Yeah. This is excellent!" agreed Lark.

Jessie smiled and continued.

"Well, as the story goes, Harriet came into Virginia's room — this very room — and she couldn't find Virginia. The girl was fourteen years old at that time — you saw the pictures downstairs. She was very pretty. Long, dark hair, slender, with beautiful posture or 'carriage' as they called it in those days, and according to letters we have of her mother's, green, green eyes. Harriet is immediately concerned when she can't find Virginia, because apparently, Virginia did not want to go on the trip at all. She was easily seasick, and she was scared of whales and the rough sailors, and she didn't want to leave her pony behind. But once Captain Hand had agreed to bring the family, he had insisted that it be the whole family; he couldn't handle the complications of leaving someone behind.

"Well, Harriet looked everywhere, all over the house, calling and calling for Virginia. But she couldn't find her. And then, suddenly, Harriet is urgently summoned up here to this very room by one of the servants. It seems Virginia had been found, but she was unconscious. She had fallen between the bed and the wall and no one had thought to check there until this servant decided to look under the bed to see if Virginia was hiding. She saw an arm."

Phoebe's neck tickled and her ears pricked as she turned to look at the far wall. Right this very minute, the girls' shadows were dancing along that same wall, cast by the flickering light from the lantern. All of a sudden, it felt a little eerie to be sleeping in this olden-days bedroom with the things that had belonged to a girl like themselves long ago. Phoebe looked around at the others. Kate had ducked her head inside her sleeping bag and was hiding. Neeve looked petrified. Lark's mouth was hanging open, and Hillary was grinning. Typical, all of them. Phoebe looked at Jessie, who was smiling, clearly pleased that her story was having the desired effect. She continued slowly, weighting each word with significance.

"Virginia was sick. Very sick. Fever, chills, nausea."

"No!" said Phoebe, shocked. "What did they do?"

"Well," said Jessie, "Captain Hand had set up the journey for his family to accompany him. Harriet had begged and begged and finally won; this illness was just the kind of reason that Captain Hand had given *against* bringing the family on board. Now, there was no question of Virginia coming. The last thing they needed was a sick person in close quarters at sea. What if she had something contagious? Harriet argued fervently with the captain, but one look at Virginia told him all he needed to know. He insisted he was leaving: Their departure time was sunup and he was going to keep to schedule. That's what captains did. Harriet and the boys could come or stay behind, as they saw fit. Harriet had only a split second to make her decision. Should she stay home with a sick child, who could potentially die or even infect Harriet and kill her, too? Or should she join her husband and sons at sea, leaving her sick child behind?"

Jessie paused, her red hair shining almost gold in the lantern light. Her eyes were wide behind her glasses, mirroring the eyes of all the cousins and Lark in their sleeping bags (except Kate, who might have actually just fallen asleep).

"What happened?" urged Phoebe.

Jessie grinned. "I'll tell you tomorrow."

"No!" screeched Phoebe in protest. "You can't! You can't leave us hanging like this! Please! I'll . . . I'll . . . I'll give you five dollars. . . ."

Jessie laughed out loud. "No. It's so much better this way. See if you can figure out what she did. Stay or go?"

"Aaah!" Phoebe moaned in protest. Jessie stood and crossed the room to turn on the hall light. "It's a great story, isn't it?" she asked rhetorically.

"Awesome," said Hillary drowsily.

"Very, very good," agreed Phoebe. She was still a little miffed though. As a reader, *she* always chose where in the story she'd stop reading; the lack of control of this story kind of bugged her. It would torture her to wait until morning to find out.

"I'm going to leave this light on out here," said Jessie, gesturing to the hall. "And I'm right across here. Please wake me up if you need anything at all. Even if it's just that you're scared." She winked and smiled again.

"Thank you so much, Jessie," said Phoebe. "This has been . . . just . . ."

"Brilliant!" offered Neeve sleepily.

"Yes. Brilliant," agreed Phoebe.

Ten thirty. Phoebe dropped her hand back to her side, glad again that her watch glowed in the dark. All around her were the even breaths of her cousins and Lark. She knew Jessie had been up reading for a while, but about half an hour ago she, too, had turned off her light, and now Phoebe knew for sure that she was the only one awake.

She was going crazy, not knowing the end of Virginia's story. Did her mother stay with her? Did she leave her, choosing her healthy husband and sons over her maybe-dying daughter? Being in the very room where it had happened made not knowing worse. And Phoebe, researcher that she was, knew that the answer was downstairs in the entrance gallery, where all of the family history was mounted on the walls and displayed in glass vitrine cases.

Phoebe rolled onto her side again. She wasn't used to going to sleep this early on vacation. Normally she'd have another two hours of reading ahead of her; her body was off schedule. She sighed noisily, hoping to wake someone up, but they slept on.

"This is ridiculous," she said out loud. Finally, without even thinking it through, she flung open her sleeping bag and stood up, grabbing the flashlight she'd put next to her sleeping bag when she'd gotten in.

She walked out of the room, not trying to be quiet, really, because she would've been happy if she'd woken someone up sort of accidentally. (She just felt weird doing it on purpose, like they'd think she was scared or something, when she wasn't.) She walked down the hall to the stairs, and turned on her flashlight. When she got downstairs, she looked in all the obvious places for the light switch to turn on the overhead light, but there wasn't one. It must've been in some big museumy panel somewhere. Sighing in annoyance, she began to make her way along the screen on which the early Hand family information was hung. Working her way photo by photo, she tried to figure out where Virginia appeared in the family narrative.

Suddenly, something caught her eye. But it wasn't in the display. She whipped her head to the side — there'd been a movement in the other room. Something light-colored had passed across her line of sight. A chill crept over Phoebe's body and she could feel the hot adrenaline course though her system all in a rush. Was it a person? A headlight from a car driving past the museum? Or was it a ghost? Phoebe couldn't decide which would be worse, something alive or something . . . dead. She stood, rooted to the spot, her eyes straining across the dark hall into the parlor until she thought they'd pop out of her head.

After what felt like an eternity but might have only been minutes, she saw it again. A person crossed the parlor. A person with long, dark hair. Tall. Good posture. A white dress. Some sort of light bed jacket and something white billowing out behind her.

An angel!

Phoebe must've cried out — in fear or happiness, it would be hard to say — before she fainted, but she didn't even hear herself. The others told her later. After she'd come to.

CHAPTER NINETEEN

Wings

It wouldn't have been so bad if Jessie hadn't insisted they call Gee, Phoebe decided later. But somehow, it took on the feeling of a tragedy or something when she arrived. Gee was a good sport about it, claiming she'd only been reading in bed when the call came anyway, but Phoebe was mortified about causing the commotion and she had a big bump on the back of her head from where she'd fallen. She couldn't remember what she'd been doing when she'd fallen. Had she been on her way to the bathroom? She wasn't sure.

At first, Jessie had thought someone had fallen down the stairs when she was jolted awake by the thud. Everyone else woke up when they heard Jessie racing down the stairs, and they quickly saw that Phoebe was missing. In any case, everyone was a little shaken. Jessie felt terrible, though.

"I am *so* sorry," she said over and over again. "I must've given you a nightmare or something with my story."

Phoebe had to comfort her. "It wasn't your fault. I'm the one who went downstairs." But she was confused. Why had she? And what had happened after that? She kept feeling like she'd seen something. But had she? Was she just sleepwalking? Dreaming? Everything was fuzzy.

Jessie assumed everyone would want to go home with Gee, but she hadn't counted on the Callahan cousins and how they always liked to finish what they started, one way or another. Hillary and Neeve insisted they were tired and they were going back up to bed. Lark followed suit, and Phoebe, having been given the all clear by Gee about the bump on her head, wanted to stay, too. Kate was desperate to go home, but didn't want to sleep in her room at The Sound alone (she felt like it would be pathetic to take Gee up on her offer to sleep in her room). In the end, they decided that Jessie would move her cot into Virginia Hand's room and they'd all be together, and Kate agreed to stay. Gee left and Jessie carefully locked the door behind them.

It took a little bit longer for everyone to settle back down again upstairs, and Jessie immediately told them the entire end of the story. It turned out that Harriet had taken a good look at Virginia and decided that the illness was not overly serious. A thorough rummage through Virginia's room turned up a foul concoction of whale oil and milk that she'd forced herself to drink in order to make herself sick, hoping to not have to go on the voyage. Harriet decided that if Virginia was truly that set against it, then her place was at home. However, she let the boys go on with their father, and six months later they all perished in a storm off the coast of South America. Virginia lived to be ninety-three years old.

"Wow," said Phoebe after Jessie finished. She rubbed the back of her head tenderly and lay there thinking about what she had seen. If only she could . . .

"Wait!" she said, sitting upright and turning up the lantern so the room was bright. "I know what happened! I saw . . . an . . . I saw Virginia! She was young and beautiful. She was wearing a long white nightgown, and her hair was loose and hanging down her back. And she crossed the parlor. That was what I saw." Relief spread through Phoebe and, at the same time, total exhaustion. She was glad she'd remembered. There was more to it, but she couldn't quite fit all the pieces together in her mind. She also thought that there was something strangely familiar about Virginia, but she wasn't going to mention that either. Not until she knew what it was.

"Spooky!" said Hillary with a giggle.

"Really, I saw her!" protested Phoebe.

"Okay, we believe you," agreed Neeve, clearly not believing.

But the novelty of sleeping in a museum coupled with the spookiness of the story Jessie had told earlier did give a wisp of possibility to Phoebe's story. Kate was actually a little scared, but after everyone laughed at her she felt better. However, Phoebe grew more and more sure of it herself, and by the time she dropped off to sleep, she remembered it all perfectly.

The next morning, the girls woke early since there were no shades on the windows of the museum and the sun was streaming in. Also, it had grown colder overnight and they were anxious to be fully dressed and moving around. Everyone was stiff and sore from their night on the floor, but in the light of day, Phoebe's dramatic story had no ring of truth to it for the others at all.

"I'm sure you just dreamt it," said Neeve, packing her things into her tote bag.

"Yeah, really, really vividly," agreed Kate, nodding her head vigorously. She couldn't even stand the idea that there might be such a thing as ghosts. She'd never sleep a wink again if that was true.

But Phoebe was sure, and she was also proud of herself. She felt like she'd been given a comforting glimpse that there was life after death; it was as if she'd been chosen to have that secret revealed to her.

Jessie was still apologetic the next morning, but the girls rallied around her to lift her spirits. They told her over and over how she'd given them one of the most memorable nights of their lives, and they wouldn't have wanted it any other way.

"After all, if it wasn't for you, I never would've seen what I saw!" Phoebe added.

"Oh golly," said Jessie ruefully. "That doesn't make me feel any better!"

Gee picked them up at eight after their breakfast snack of angel cake and orange juice from a thermos. Phoebe headed upstairs for a nap in her own bed, and the others hung out downstairs with Gee and Sheila and filled them in on all the details of the overnight.

When Phoebe awoke again, everyone was gearing up to go Christmas shopping in town, so she grabbed a quick bite and joined them.

Town was cold again. Truly cold. And Phoebe was pleased about that. The girls split up and branched out across town to buy presents for each other. Phoebe had the little pins already, so she was just going to get one more little thing for everyone. She'd give Gee the pomanders she'd made, and she picked up two packs of shin-high cushiony athletic socks for Hillary, who was always complaining that her socks were trashed. For Neeve she selected a wild chiffon scarf from Gull Boutique that Neeve could probably use in myriad ways Phoebe would never dream of. For Kate, the obvious choice was yarn. Phoebe selected a rich, raspberry pink but double-checked with the counter girl at the Old Mill to make sure Kate could exchange it if she didn't like it. For Sheila she picked up rose-scented foot salts at the pharmacy, and for Lark, whom she'd forgotten before, she got a new rope bracelet to match theirs. She also picked out a pretty holiday candle for Mrs. Bradshaw and dropped it off at Summer Reading with a card thanking Mrs. Bradshaw for her help with Gee's "present."

With everything accomplished, Phoebe was free to indulge herself for another half an hour, so she decided to sit and look at books at Summer Reading until it was time to meet the others. It was a slow, quiet day, but it was a balm for Phoebe's soul after the night she'd had. She tried not to think about the . . . thing she'd seen downstairs at the museum, but every few minutes it flitted across her consciousness and she struggled to keep it at bay. She selected an angel book she hadn't already bought, and then she sat down in one of the big armchairs with the book in her lap. Looking down at the cover, the vision from last night suddenly swam into her head, complete.

There *had* been something familiar about what she'd seen, and now it struck her like a lightening bolt. The angel from Gee's tree! The one she'd broken! That was what it looked like! It — Virginia, or whoever — had had wings! White wings trailing out behind her!

Ooh! She shivered in broad daylight, right there in Summer Reading. So it was an angel. A smile bloomed on her face. She'd seen an angel. Her very own angel! How lucky could one person get? She couldn't possibly tell the others. They'd think she'd gone crackers for sure. But maybe Gee? Or Farren? She'd have to see.

Phoebe rubbed her arms briskly to warm up the goosebumps that had risen on her skin. She'd known the sleepover would be special, that this whole trip would be special, but she'd had no idea. And now this. She had been given the gift of faith, and peace, and she couldn't imagine a lovelier present in the world.

That night, after an early dinner, Lark and Mr. Kendo came to pick the girls up for caroling. Gee stood at the door, her arms hugging herself against the chill wind that was now blowing steadily across the sound.

"Only an hour, girls," Gee had warned. "It's cold, you had a late night last night, and we have the party tomorrow. I don't want anyone getting overtired or sick for Christmas."

An hour wasn't very long, but it was better than nothing. Phoebe thought Gee might've revoked her permission for them to go caroling — in fact, she'd almost hoped Gee would. But Neeve, in particular, was so excited to go that it seemed cruel not to go. Phoebe was privately aglow at having been honored by the vision from the night before, and she would've done anything for someone else, just in gratitude for her gift.

They bounced into town in Mr. Kendo's SUV, and were happy to see a whole gang of kids — about twenty of them — gathered at the Lost at Sea memorial, just as planned. The girls raced across the village green, looking for friends, and they found them. Talbot was there, and Atticus, and Andrea and Tessa from clinic, and a few other people they knew a little and liked well enough. Mr. Kendo was meeting them back at that exact spot in fifty minutes and everyone had synchronized their watches. About five minutes after the girls arrived, the carolers set off for the residential streets of town, singing as they walked.

Phoebe's emotions were running high, but there was an undeniable joy and unity to the group of kids that was very uplifting. She couldn't stop thinking about the angel now, and she felt so special and singled out that it had appeared to her, that her usual emotional defenses were cracking. Adding the music to that, sentimental and beautiful as much of it was, Phoebe found herself actually getting a tiny bit teary here and there.

It started with "Silent Night," happened again with "The Little Drummer Boy," and by the time they sang "Angels We Have Heard On High," Phoebe was really — for her — worked up. She could've actually burst into tears. Here she was, having the Christmas she'd always dreamed of, and now an angel had visited her, she was getting a dog for Gee, they were having a big party tomorrow, it was cold. Everything was absolutely perfect, and she was grateful.

The carolers were walking and singing mostly, but whenever they reached the house of either someone in the group, or someone's friend who had not yet come out, they'd stop and sing until the door opened and people either joined them, or brought out treats, like candy canes or chocolates.

Soon enough, Phoebe realized they were heading for Sloan's house, and they stopped right outside. Looking around, Phoebe realized Sloan was not with them yet, and someone must've been trying to draw her out to join them. Phoebe could not bring herself to sing. The last thing she wanted was for Sloan to come join them. They were working their way quickly through "Deck the Halls," and there was still no sign of Sloan or anyone in her family, even though the house was brightly lit. But just as they reached the last stanza of "Fa la la la la," Phoebe saw something that made her gasp.

Someone in a light-colored jacket had crossed in front of the front hall window while throwing a white scarf on across her shoulders. The person had long dark hair. She was tall, with good posture, and the scarf billowed out behind her like wings.

Sloan.

No! It couldn't have been! Phoebe knew what she'd seen last night and it had been . . . ghostly! Not flesh and blood!

But cold logic took over. Phoebe's bubble was burst, and all of her holiday cheer switched off like Christmas tree lights being suddenly unplugged. She wasn't special. She hadn't seen an angel. She'd seen Sloan trying to sneak in on their sleepover was what she'd seen. What an idiot she'd been! As if an angel would just appear like that, at a sleepover. Phoebe was so mad at herself for getting all hyped up that all of her newfound faith and peace dissipated. There couldn't be such a thing as angels. They were just tacky mug decorations. They weren't real! Heck, even if they were, why would one of them suddenly appear to *her*? It was just too good to be true!

Angrily, Phoebe turned on her heel and began walking

quickly away from the group. At first, the cousins and Lark didn't see her go. She was so mad at herself for believing and at Sloan for sneaking into the museum, that she felt energized enough to walk all the way back to The Sound on foot. But she heard running footsteps behind her, and suddenly the cousins were all around her and she was crying, bawling, as if she'd never cried before (it had been quite a while since she'd cried), and there'd be no walking home alone.

CHAPTER TWENTY

Blizzard

$\mathcal{T}$ucked into her bed after a warm bath, with an empty mug of chamomile tea at her bedside, Phoebe was drowsy and relaxed. After Phoebe's breakdown, or whatever, Neeve had raced back to find Talbot in the crowd and use his cell phone to call Gee to come and get them. Phoebe had been totally overwrought by the time Gee arrived, and the cousins and Lark were frankly glad to have an adult in charge. They'd quickly dropped Lark at home to explain what had happened, and then they'd gone home and let Gee take over.

Phoebe stopped crying after a half an hour or so, and when she came out of her bath, she told Gee everything she could think of. Starting with the Proper Christmas file (which she'd gone and gotten for Gee to look at), through the sledding, Mrs. Merrihew's gaffe, the angel books, her new belief, and the bazaar, to the sleepover and Sloan's cameo appearance that had touched off Phoebe's whole fainting incident. She also mentioned the fact that she didn't ever cry because she was so deeply terrified of dying and what happened after and everything that she worried that if she started crying she'd never stop. Losing her belief in angels made her go for broke; nothing else mattered anymore.

Gee had brought the tea, listened closely, admired the clippings in Phoebe's file, smiled at certain parts of Phoebe's monologue, hugged at certain parts (Phoebe was wrung out enough to accept a hug gratefully), and generally made Phoebe feel understood and better by the time she'd finished talking.

"Okay," said Gee afterward, taking a deep breath and placing her hands on her knees, businesslike. "There's no need for a huge lecture from me. For starters, let's just dismiss any of the Sloan craziness. Any time she's involved, emotions run very high. I'm sorry for you and the others that she spooked you at the sleepover, but, come to think of it, I wouldn't have expected any less. In fact," Gee corrected herself, laughing, "I'd have expected more!"

Phoebe managed a wan smile, too, just thinking of the evil things Sloan could have dreamt up to destroy their sleepover.

"Okay, moving on, I think it's clear to both of us that you are brilliantly smart and sensitive, and you have gotten yourself in way over your head with some of your reading material and your thinking." She tilted her head to the side and smiled at Phoebe until Phoebe reluctantly nodded in agreement. She didn't necessarily agree that she was brilliant, but she understood what Gee was getting at.

"Now. You are far too young to worry so much about death and dying, although I personally do find, at my age, that angel stories and church and prayer and all of that *are* enormously comforting and satisfying. You have decades before you need to worry about the afterlife, and I don't want you wasting any time on that now, understand? Now I think you should take a bit of a break from all that maudlin drama and save it for a rainy day somewhere down the line, alright?"

"Yes," said Phoebe. It was true. Those angel stories had really made her a little crazy.

"However, I don't think you should throw the baby out with the bathwater. If the angels afforded you comfort — about the afterlife or heaven or whatever — then I think you should just go on believing. You don't have to have proof to believe; that's why it's called a leap of faith. Believing in angels or heaven is the best gamble you could ever take. After all, what do you have to lose?"

Phoebe nodded. She could try. Maybe not today, but in a little while.

"Additionally, I think you've put a huge amount of pressure on yourself and on this Christmas in general for everything to be perfect. I understand where you're coming from, and I do find some of your parents' traditions a little, ah, *un*traditional. But you can't deny that they are working hard to make things fun and unique for you girls, and to spend time together as a family, and with friends, and that's the true spirit of Christmas."

Again, Phoebe nodded.

"Here on my end, I'll do everything in my power to make the rest of this Christmas picture-perfect for you. You deserve a real Currier and Ives type of Christmas and, except for making it snow, I can give you that."

Phoebe started to protest, but Gee hushed her. "Just let me. But most importantly, I want you to focus on taking care of yourself, and truly enjoying yourself. Christmas is treated nowadays as a stress-inducing checklist, and if you let yourself get swept up in that mindset, it's just not joyful. Eggnog, check. Presents, check. Carols, check. Tree, check. Are we having fun yet?"

Phoebe giggled.

"That's what I like to see!" Gee reached over and patted Phoebe on the knee. "Just take it easy on yourself, Phoebe Callahan. Life is not perfect, and no one expects you to be perfect either. Let your guard down a little. Cry. Hug. Once in a while, choose to go do something that's slightly imperfect instead of reading about people doing things perfectly." Gee winked. "Get it?"

"Got it."

"Good."

Phoebe sighed. "Thanks, Gee. Not just for this but for this whole vacation, for everything. Summer, too."

"I can honestly say that it has been entirely my pleasure, Miss Callahan," Gee said with a grin. "Now I think you need to scoot and get a good night's sleep. We have a big, fancy, imperfect Christmas party to throw tomorrow."

"Bee! *Phoebe*! Wake up!" It was Hillary. Phoebe was dreaming that they had to go on a whaling ship and Hillary was waking her up but she didn't want to go. She rolled over and pulled the blankets up high over her shoulder. "No!" she muttered vehemently, still half-asleep.

"Phoe-*be*! It's snowing *sideways*! You have to *see* this!"

Now Phoebe was awake. She half-sat up and looked at her watch. *Ack!* Only eight-thirty. Her eyelids felt leaden and sticky; she could go back to sleep for two more hours!

But *snow*!

"Bee!" Hillary started again.

"I'm awake!" growled Phoebe.

"Good," grinned Hillary. *"It's beginning to look a lot like Christmas!"* she sang.

"Everywhere we go!" came Kate's muffled soprano from across the hall.

"It's inhuman to sing like that first thing in the morning," said Phoebe grouchily, but she climbed out of bed and came to stand at the window next to Hillary. What she saw jolted her right awake.

"It's a white-out!" announced Hillary.

Phoebe's jaw dropped in astonishment.

Kate and Neeve burst into the room, just as they had only a few days earlier. "It's snowing, it's snowing!" they chanted.

Phoebe was mesmerized. She couldn't tear her eyes away

from the sight. Everything was covered in white. Bushes were white lumps. You couldn't distinguish the driveway from the lawn. The sky was entirely white, and white flakes filled the air.

"Wow," she murmured.

"I hope it stops snowing in time for the caterers to get here," said Kate over Phoebe's shoulder.

"Yeah. Me, too," said Phoebe, astounded. She hadn't even thought of that.

But of course it didn't. The girls had half-dressed and hustled downstairs to find out the weather report from Gee, and they discovered Sheila and Gee huddled around the television in the sewing room. The weatherman was coyly saying he didn't want to use the *B* word yet, and Sheila was yelling at him in frustration.

"Go on, you coward! Say it! Blizzard!" She was shaking her fist in the air at him and huffing and puffing. It was the most riled up Phoebe had ever seen her, and she thought Sheila might actually blow a gasket.

"All that food," Sheila was saying. "Got to try to get it to keep."

Aha! Sheila was worried about wasting the food. But . . . why would the food be wasted unless . . .

"Gee?" said Phoebe, wheeling around in shock. "Is our party canceled?" Phoebe knew her eyes were big and round with dismay and she didn't try to hide it. Gee paused and put her hand on Phoebe's cheek.

"Phoebe, my dear, they're calling for at least six more inches. Somehow, I just don't think people are going to want to be out driving in this tonight. Especially not when the temperature drops, later." She chuckled. "And especially not with any of Sheila's eggnog in them."

"So what do we do?" wailed Phoebe.

"We call everyone and let them off the hook by postponing the party for tomorrow night," answered Gee.

"Tomorrow?" Phoebe brightened. "That's not so bad. So we can just have the same exact party tomorrow night instead?" she asked.

"Well, I don't know about the same exact. I expect it will be smaller, as some people have plans already and won't be able to join us. And it will be more casual, as I know the caterers won't be available. They'll be doing the Durkins' big bash up the island like they always do."

"So what will we do?" asked Phoebe pathetically.

"We'll just let people help themselves to drinks, and we'll put out the food instead of passing it, and we'll have a wonderful time."

"But why is Sheila worried about the food going bad?" Sheila had stormed into the kitchen and Phoebe could hear her in there now, opening and shutting cabinets and the door to the fridge, muttering to herself.

"Um, I'm not sure how to say this, but, here goes. Every time we've ever had a blizzard on Gull, the power has gone out. And that means no refrigerator."

"Blast! And we can't put stuff outside?" asked Phoebe.

"Well, not things that can't freeze, like cooked shrimp and cheese and things."

"So we won't have any light either?" asked Kate worriedly.

"Well, I'm going now to call Mr. Addison and see if he can get the generator going. Then we can run the heat and some of the lights so we can at least stay warm and watch the weather reports, and have a few lights here and there."

"Bummer." Phoebe stared out over the white lawn. She couldn't actually even see the lawn. The snow was so dense she could only see about ten feet from the house. *Be careful what you wish for,* she thought to herself. *White Christmas. Ha!*

CHAPTER TWENTY-ONE

Power

They were all sitting in the sewing room, eating a dinner of hors d'oeuvres that would have spoiled if they had waited until the next day. Deviled eggs that would've gone dry, and shrimp that would've turned fishy, but was right now absolutely delicious. Phoebe was watching the TV, totally engrossed, so luckily, she wasn't the one who saw Sloan first. If she had been, she probably would've fainted all over again.

It was Hillary who saw her, although she didn't realize who it was at first. She heard the bang on the window, and looked up to see Sloan's face hovering inches from her own. Hillary wasn't a shrieker, but she did shout in surprise, and all at once the room of passive TV watchers came alive. Gee rushed to the door to let Sloan in, and Sheila hurried to prepare hot tea and something warm to eat. Phoebe dashed upstairs for dry clothes, and when she came back down, Sloan was shivering in a blanket on the couch, telling her story.

She hadn't gotten the message that the party was canceled because she'd been working at the store all morning — there had been a huge rush on food and other staples, like flashlights and batteries. Everyone had known the power would go. So by the time Sloan had gotten home, the power was, of course, out, and she hadn't even thought there might be a message on the machine for her.

She hadn't wanted to miss out on the party. She knew from previous experience that Callahan parties were a blast, but her parents had refused to bring her, and their phones were all electric so she couldn't call. Therefore, she'd waited until her parents had gotten engrossed in a radio program, and she'd snuck out and cross-country skied over.

Gee immediately went to call the police station to see if they could get one of the plow drivers over to the Bickets to let them know what had happened. Meanwhile, despite her dash for clothes (which had been merely instinctive), Phoebe was disgusted by Sloan's presence. After all she'd put Phoebe through the other night, Phoebe wasn't as ready to forgive and forget as the other cousins clearly were. They wanted to hear all about Sloan's adventure getting to their house, and all about what town had been like today, with people who'd blown off their last-minute Christmas food shopping struggling to haul turkeys and things out to their cars for Christmas Eve dinner tomorrow.

When Gee returned from the kitchen, she announced that Sloan had better sleep over, and Neeve, to Phoebe's dismay, actually cheered. But the look on Sloan's face when Neeve cheered almost made Phoebe soften a bit. Almost. Sloan had worn a look of pure joy and happiness, as well as surprise that someone should make such a happy fuss over her.

Gee came and sat down next to Phoebe, and she whispered in Phoebe's ear. "I have a present from your parents that I'd been saving, but I think it might be fun to open it and use it tonight. I just want you to come see it and give your permission."

Only Hillary caught Gee whispering, and she looked quizzically at Phoebe as Phoebe stood to follow Gee out of the room. Phoebe shrugged, just as clueless as Hillary, and went to see what it was.

Gee had brought a flashlight, and as they crossed through the living room, the beam of the flashlight bobbed on the floor ahead of them as they walked. When they got to the sun porch, Gee laid her shoulder against the always-stuck door and shoved it open. Then she reached in with one arm to drag a box toward her.

A blast of chillier air filled the room; the porch was insulated but with its brick floor and all the french doors, it was always way cooler than the rest of the house, especially in the winter.

"Here, Gee. Let me help," offered Phoebe.

Gee stood to the side while Phoebe grabbed the curious box and lifted it out. Gee then closed the door and Phoebe put the box on the floor. It was about two feet high, and around fourteen inches in every other direction, and it was wrapped in the tackiest Christmas gift wrap Phoebe had ever seen, from what she could make out in the dim illumination provided by the flashlight.

She rolled her eyes in the dark and wryly said, "I can only imagine."

"I know what it is," said Gee with a smile in her voice that Phoebe could hear rather than see. "Go on. Open it."

Phoebe pulled the paper off the sides of the box and let it fall to the floor. "It's some kind of electronic . . . like a boom box? Oh. Oh no. No." And Phoebe started to laugh really, really hard.

It was a karaoke machine.

"Don't you love it?" asked Gee, laughing, too. "After all your talk the other night, it arrived the next day with a note addressed to me. Your dad said he thought you'd probably be really upset to miss their annual karaoke carols party, and would I please make sure that you and the cousins had a chance to use this so his little Bee wouldn't get too homesick."

Now Phoebe was roaring, and the sound of her laughter brought the others in. It was starting to seem that if Phoebe wasn't hysterically crying, she was hysterically laughing these days.

"What? What is it?" the cousins were clamoring for an answer.

"Oh! Oh!" Phoebe's laughter was dying down and she was trying to get her bearings again.

"Go on. You tell them, sweetheart," urged Gee.

Phoebe waited for a tantalizing moment until she knew they were all about to die of curiosity. "It's a karaoke machine!" she cried.

The girls burst out laughing and then Sloan, who had followed them into the living room, asked, "What? What did I miss?" And Kate filled her in on the joke.

It wasn't fifteen minutes before they had the thing fired up, and Phoebe was doing a brilliant rendition of "Grandma Got Run Over by a Reindeer" that had everyone's sides aching with laughter all over again.

"My family is never this fun," stated Sloan, who was clearly feeling that her trek had been worth it.

And for the next hour and a half, they gorged themselves on Christmas party snacks and belted out horrible Christmas songs.

Finally, with teeth all brushed and pj's on (borrowed ones for Sloan), the girls dove into their beds. It hadn't been the day that Phoebe had expected, but it had turned out fun in its own way. Now Sloan was sleeping in their room because it had a little armchair that pulled out into a futon. Phoebe wasn't particularly psyched about this arrangement. She'd been looking forward to discussing Sloan with Hillary behind a closed door, and anyway, Neeve and Kate were the ones who were such big Sloan fans. She should've been sleeping across the hall. But there hadn't been a graceful way for Phoebe to kick Sloan out, so she was stuck.

Lying in her own bed, in her own room (at least her own for while she was on Gull), Phoebe grew more and more enraged by Sloan's presence. She started to huff, and toss and turn, flouncing her covers ostentatiously.

Finally, Sloan asked, "Are you feeling alright, Phoebe?"

Phoebe hadn't been sure that Sloan was still awake, but she knew Hillary was asleep. She could really say anything that she wanted to Sloan right now in the dark and no one would ever know. She wouldn't even have to see Sloan's face crumple.

"No, as a matter of fact, I am not feeling alright. The bump on my head is still killing me and I am exhausted from the drama at the sleepover the other night, and I can't believe you had the nerve to turn up here tonight after everything!" Phoebe was breathing hard. She didn't know where to go next with her diatribe. It would depend on Sloan's reaction to the fact that Phoebe knew she'd been at the museum that night.

"Wow. Um. O-*kay*. . . ."

"Oh, quit stalling, Bicket!" snarled Phoebe, but quietly, so as not to wake Hillary.

"Fine. I am sorry to hear about your head, and that's too bad that you didn't get enough sleep at the sleepover, but it's not like it's my fault! And I turned up here tonight because *you invited* me!"

"Wait, back up a second there, sweetheart," said Phoebe sarcastically. "You're saying the head injury isn't your fault? And the fact that I didn't sleep all that night? What, so sneaking around other people's sleepovers and making them faint with fear and then having my grandmother have to come because of it all, you think that's a no-fault kind of thing?" Now Phoebe was worked up. Hillary snorted in her sleep and rolled onto her back, and Phoebe glanced at her nervously in the dark.

"What the heck are you talking about? Have you gone totally crazy?" demanded Sloan.

And just then, the power came back on and the room was illuminated in total brightness. Sloan was standing next to her futon, her hands out in the air in a question, and Phoebe was kneeling in her mattress, her nightgown hiked up around her knees. They both blinked at the shock of the light, and Phoebe shaded her eyes from the unaccustomed glare.

"Have *I* gone crazy?" she asked calmly. "*I* am the victim here!"

"Listen, you, you, *weirdo*. I wasn't at your dumb little museum sleepover the other night! I was on the mainland at my stupid cousin Jeremy's Christmas pageant with my parents!" Sloan's eyes flashed with anger, and Phoebe collapsed back on her heels in shock.

"The mainland?" She reached up and twisted her hair into a tight bun while she processed this new information. "So . . . that wasn't you?"

Sloan shook her head. "If you saw someone you thought was me that night, sister, it wasn't. You can call my parents if you don't believe me."

"Then. . . . Who was it?"

Chapter Twenty-two

The Pickup

$\mathcal{P}$hoebe awoke Christmas Eve morning with cobwebs of disbelief still clinging to the far reaches of her mind. She had spent the rest of the night telling Sloan the story of the sleepover, then convincing herself that she had been sleepwalking and had simply dreamed the apparition. Or maybe . . . not? Her sleep, when it came, was fitful and she did not awake rested, but the day held high expectations of her.

The snow had tapered off through the previous evening and now the sky was clear, and blue, and hard-looking, without a cloud in sight. The windows were rattling in their casements as the strong wind kept up, and the snow lifted in the yard in little swirling eddies, all the flakes glinting diamond-like in the sun. Out the big window in the kitchen, the sound was navy blue, almost black, and the white caps appeared to race across it like shorn wool from a lamb blowing across the hard-packed earth of a barnyard. When Gee went out to see if the roads were passable (she'd shockingly skipped her swim that morning, which was a first for the girls to witness), the back door had brought in a gust of wind so strong and cold that it had left Phoebe, who was standing nearby, breathless.

The phone began ringing around nine thirty, with calls from party guests, most of whom were accepting. The kitchen raged with activity as Sheila scrambled to concoct hors d'oeuvres that would make use of the things that were left and would be easy for the girls to help prepare and serve; they probably wouldn't be able to get much of their order from Callie's Cupboard, if anything at all.

Phoebe was so busy she hardly noticed the time, and with meals served catch-as-catch-can on the counter, there wasn't any real structure to mark the passing of the day. Before she knew it, they were hustling upstairs to change into their party clothes — a long green velvet skirt for Phoebe, with a white, cap-sleeved silky blouse, and an array of other dressy things for the cousins. Gee had instructed guests to dress casually, as it was no fun trudging through ten inches of snow in dressy clothes, but the girls had all wanted to wear what they'd planned for the night before, when the party was still fancy.

Sloan had somehow stuck around for the day, proving herself surprisingly useful in the kitchen, and Phoebe's shock from the previous night had completely dissipated any anger she felt toward Sloan. At the moment she was neutral, but it could still go either way. However, in the spirit of Christmas, she lent Sloan some clothes, and Sloan was appropriately gracious and grateful, and this mollified Phoebe even further.

When Phoebe got back downstairs, two caterers had arrived, sent on the plowed roads by the Durkins who had felt bad about Gee's party plight (she had had to uninvite them for the night before and was now missing their party to host her own). Nigel and Carlos had come to Gee's rescue, and had already busied themselves by setting up a bar, lighting fires in the fireplaces in the dining room and living room, and laying the gorgeous antique tablecloth and napkins out on the dining room table for the buffet. Even if the hors d'oeuvres were to be simplified, their presentation would not.

In fact, Phoebe didn't see anything that looked casual or like a compromise, as Gee had described the night before. The tree in the living room was lit and stunning; joyful string music played just a little bit loudly on the speakers of the stereo system; wonderful smells wafted from the kitchen, joined by the smell of melting wax from all the decorative Christmas candles and a whiff of the woodsmoke from the fires; and Phoebe felt that she was experiencing the most essential Christmas ever. Best of all, Sheila had given the girls an early Christmas present: A gingerbread house she'd made and decorated from scratch. It now sat in the middle of the buffet looking both regal and scrumptious.

She paused in the living room to admire all the decorations, and thought how lucky she was. She had a kind of nutty but loving family back home, three special cousins among many and an amazing grandmother, a pile of newish friends about to arrive, nice gifts she was looking forward to giving out tomorrow (the dog! She couldn't stop thinking about the dog!), and a beautiful setting in which to celebrate Christmas. And then the doorbell rang and interrupted her moment of gratitude, and the party had started.

An hour and a half later, Phoebe checked her watch. It was ten to eight and it was time for her to go get her outdoor clothes on to head down to the bottom of the driveway and meet the Bradshaws with the puppy. She had called them earlier to make sure they could proceed with their plan tonight, and the cover of the party made things much easier. Phoebe was almost starting to think they should just give the dog to Gee tonight. After all, lots of people opened one gift on Christmas Eve.

Without ceremony, she slipped away from the party and out to the kitchen, where she rolled up her skirt to keep it out of the snow, jammed on her snow boots, and bundled into her coat. Sheila gave her a funny look but said nothing; she was too swamped at the island to really care what Phoebe was doing. Phoebe opened the door, struggling to close it behind her in the blasting wind, and crossed the front of the house quickly, so Gee wouldn't see her if she opened the front door for more guests.

Luckily people were coming and going and parked all up

and down the driveway and road, so she didn't stick out. She reached the bottom of the driveway and looked around, her hands jammed in her coat pockets, wishing she'd worn her hat. And then the headlights in a jeep flickered; this was their planned signal (it was all very James Bond), and Phoebe jogged lightly across the snow to the vehicle. Mr. and Mrs. Bradshaw climbed out, and Mr. Bradshaw reached back in behind him and pulled out a soft, suitcaselike dog carrier. Phoebe could hear the yipping and yapping already and she knew the dog wouldn't stay quiet in the house. It would have to be tonight.

Thanking the Bradshaws profusely, Phoebe ducked her head to look in the carrier. "Hi, little fella! Merry Christmas!"

At the top of the driveway, they split up, with the Bradshaws going to the front door and Phoebe and the puppy heading for the kitchen door. Phoebe planned to scoot through the kitchen with the bag kind of hidden by her side (she hadn't worked this part of the plan out yet very well), and deposit him upstairs to wait until after the party was over.

She reached the back porch, climbed the step and, looking both ways, took a deep breath and rapidly opened the door and shut it behind her. Then she flung aside the green velvet curtain and came face to face with Gee.

"Hello, Phoebe," said Gee calmly, with a wry smile on her face. "And what do we have here?"

Phoebe was paralyzed, rooted to the spot, and the only thing to do was come clean. "Your Christmas present?" she said hopefully, holding out the bag to Gee.

Just then the puppy barked and it caught Gee by surprise. She jumped and put her hand to her chest. "My, I'd forgotten how noisy they were."

Phoebe was confused. Why wasn't Gee more surprised? "Wait," said Phoebe. "Did you know?"

"I had an inkling," said Gee sagely. "Then a conversation with some concerned cousins the other morning led me to make an inquiring phone call or two. Or three. And here we are." Gee shook her head slowly from side to side. Distractedly, Phoebe noticed that the kitchen was empty. Maybe Gee had shooed out Sheila and the caterers so she could yell at Phoebe in private. Phoebe winced.

"Come. Let's sit. I think he'll be okay in there for a moment." *Gosh, she even knows he's a boy,* thought Phoebe. *There are no surprises here.*

Phoebe and Gee sat down at the kitchen table, and Phoebe gently placed the dog's carrier on the floor next to her.

Gee put her elbow on the table and rested her cheek in her palm while she looked at Phoebe. Phoebe shifted nervously in her seat. Was Gee ever going to say something?

"The other girls told me you've wanted a puppy every Christmas for your whole life," she said finally, in a quiet voice.

Tears sprang to Phoebe's eyes and she dashed them away, annoyed. She nodded.

"A golden retriever," stated Gee. And Phoebe nodded again. The tears welled up and spilled over, and the puppy gave a sharp little bark. "Shh!" comforted Phoebe, bending down to pat the carrier. Gee smiled.

"Do you know I think it's the loveliest present anyone has ever gotten me?" she asked.

Phoebe laughed through her tears in surprise. "You haven't even seen him yet!" she protested.

"I don't need to," said Gee. "What I treasure most about the gift is that this is the singlemost thing you've ever wanted for *yourself*, and instead of spending your whole vacation here trying to figure out how to *get* it, you've spent your whole vacation trying to figure out how to *give* it, and I think that's lovely." Now Gee had tears in her eyes, too. "The only problem," she continued, "is that I really don't want a dog." She looked at Phoebe carefully. Phoebe was stock-still, the tears spilling down her face. "And you do."

Gee laid her hands flat on the table and examined them disaffectedly. "So," she said, and she looked at Phoebe.

"So," said Phoebe. Gee seemed to be waiting for Phoebe to make the next move. "So . . . Sloan wants him," she said, finally, shrugging. "And her parents said she could have him." *Whatever,* she told herself. *Sloan will be thrilled, anyway.*

Gee was still quiet. And then a smile slowly spread across her face, growing wider until it encompassed her eyes and eyebrows and nearly her ears. "So did yours," she said.

CHAPTER TWENTY-THREE

Gabriel

Gabriel was wiggling and climbing all up and down the front of Phoebe's down jacket, which she still hadn't removed, and his kisses were tickling her in one place while his tail wagged and tickled her in another. Gee was sitting at the table with her, the huge, joyful smile still on her face. Just watching Phoebe play with him.

"You know, Phoebe, I don't think I've seen you this . . . this . . . *animated* in more than a year," Gee said happily. And just then, the cousins came tearing into the kitchen, followed closely by Lark and Sloan.

"We saw the Bradshaws. . . ." said Kate breathlessly.

"Did you tell her . . . ?" asked Neeve, her face wreathed in smiles.

"Yes!" cried Phoebe. "She told me!"

It turned out that the cousins had spilled the beans during Phoebe's nap, and then the Bradshaws had confirmed what the girls had told Gee. Gee checked in with Farren, just to tie up all the loose ends, and Farren had been hugely relieved by the call. She'd been dreading a "harsh scene" on Christmas morning and had been on the verge of telling Gee about the plan herself. So Gee paid a visit to the Bradshaws, met Gabriel (for that was the name Phoebe had instantly chosen — in honor of the archangel who appears to Mary in the Bible), and was informed by Mrs. Bradshaw that she'd watched Phoebe with the puppies, just to make sure she was mature enough to handle herself around them, and had been bowled over by Phoebe's way with them. The pups had loved her, she'd been gentle and responsible, but still playful, and she'd conducted all of the phone calls and details of the transfer all on her own.

Armed with this information, Gee called Phoebe's parents and pled her case. It was unclear what it took to get them to change their minds about a puppy, but Gee told Phoebe the dog was to be hers entirely. Her parents would help out with the bills, and drive Phoebe and the dog to the vet when need be, but Phoebe would be responsible for every other aspect of his care, including finding him a place to stay when they traveled, or he'd have to go. Phoebe thought these terms were fair, and Gee insisted that the entire family would fall in love with him as soon as they met him and would soon be fighting over the chance to take him for walks.

Phoebe had a hard time imagining that, but she did have to jump out of her chair to give Gee a hug and thank her for getting her the dog.

Now, the girls wanted Phoebe to bring the puppy out to meet the party guests, and she complied. Mr. and Mrs. Bicket were among the first people she showed him to, and Sloan turned pouty and sullen when they petted him.

"You see? Her parents let her have a dog! They trust her!" she said in a low tone.

Phoebe was shocked. Hadn't Sloan said her parents wanted her to get this very dog?

But no, her mother was saying, "Sloan, with the antiques we have, a dog is just not a good idea. Those pieces are investments, darling. Now, when you grow up and have your own house . . ."

Phoebe suddenly felt so bad for Sloan that she had to turn away. She knew Sloan would have a nice Christmas even without a puppy, but still. And it was a shock to realize she'd been *had* by yet another one of Sloan's lies! *Oh well, I'm not alone,* thought Phoebe happily. *The Bradshaws were had, too!*

The front door opened and it was Jessie and her boyfriend, who was visiting from Boston. Jessie looked beautiful in an electric blue sequined sleeveless blouse ("Vintage," she admitted when Neeve admired it hungrily), and she proffered a package to Phoebe when she came in.

Phoebe laughed as she tried to take it. Gabriel scrambled to get down, outraged that his cozy perch was being disturbed, and Jessie took him from Phoebe, insisting that Phoebe open the present.

"I just felt so bad about the other night, I had to give this to you. I'd picked it up at the Christmas bazaar the other morning because I like to have a few gifts on hand during the holidays for whatever comes up, and when I thought of it I knew you had to have it."

Phoebe unwrapped the green tissue expectantly. She loved presents and she couldn't imagine from its shape what it might be. She unwound the tissue once, twice, and then the object spun into her hand. "Oh!" gasped Phoebe.

It was an angel ornament, just like the one from Gee's tree that Phoebe had broken — identical in fact, although the features were slightly different — and it was newer-looking, and a little smaller. It had long dark hair, blue eyes, a burlap dress, and wings of muslin. It was also what, or who, she'd seen at the museum the other night.

Phoebe lifted her head and stared at Jessie in shock. "Where did you say you got this?"

"Oh, from a lady who had a table full of angel things at the church bazaar the other day. Really pretty stuff."

"I bought something there, too!' said Phoebe. "I'd like to track her down. She had some things I'd like to buy more of."

Jessie was nodding, looking down at the puppy and then back at the ornament in Phoebe's hand.

"But how did you know?" Phoebe asked quietly. If Jessie hadn't been expecting the question, she wouldn't have ever heard it.

Phoebe looked up and met Jessie's eyes.

"Because you aren't the only one who's seen her," Jessie answered quietly.

Before Phoebe could recover from her shock, Gee was at her side, greeting Jessie and the boyfriend and chattering along. Phoebe looked at Jessie in a daze, wishing they could talk more, but Jessie shrugged helplessly.

"Oh, what's that you've got there, sweet pea?" asked Gee, lifting the glasses from the chain on her neck to inspect the angel ornament. "My!" she said in surprise, and she lowered her glasses to look at Phoebe, then Jessie, then back at Phoebe. "It's just like the one . . ."

"That I broke?" offered Phoebe with a guilty grin.

"Yes. Quite like it," said Gee. She put her glasses back on and took the ornament from Phoebe's hand to get a better look. "And in all these years I've never seen another."

Jessie told her the story of the angel lady at the bazaar, and Gee called over Mrs. Hagan to show it to her.

"Who was the vendor with the angels?" Gee asked Mrs. Hagan, and Mrs. Hagan looked at her in confusion.

"Angels?" she repeated. "There wasn't anyone with angels."

Jessie and Phoebe looked at each other and laughed. "No, come on, Mrs. Hagan. You know. That lady with the whole table full of angel mugs, pins, ornaments. Right before the bead table?"

But Mrs. Hagan was shaking her head. "I'll have to go back and look at my records, but we never signed someone on to sell angel stuff. I'm sure of it. Or I would've stopped to buy a few things for my sister-in-law. She collects angels." Mrs. Hagan smiled.

Neeve was passing with a fresh ginger ale from the bar, and Phoebe stopped her. "Do you remember that lady selling the angel stuff at the Christmas bazaar? You know, the one right before the bead table?"

But Neeve was already shaking her head from side to side, as Phoebe had somehow expected she would. "Uh-uh. Never saw that. And I would've noticed because . . ."

Jessie and Phoebe looked at each other and laughed incredulously.

"Who knows?" said Jessie with a shrug.

"Maybe it's like dog whistles. Maybe only certain people can see angels," laughed Phoebe.

"You know," Gee was saying as she studied the ornament again. "*This* one *does* look quite like me."

Before they left the party with their parents that night, Phoebe gave Lark and Sloan the guardian angel pins she'd originally bought for Gee and Sheila.

"Merry Christmas," she'd said, hugging one girl and then the other. Something about getting the dog had softened her up inside, and she was feeling warm and grateful to everyone, and laughing quite a lot.

Sloan accepted it shyly and said she hadn't bought Phoebe a present yet because she hadn't been able to do her last-minute shopping this year, and they all laughed. The cousins would see Lark and Sloan, if not at church the next morning (Gee having deemed midnight mass "out of the question" this year, for a variety of reasons, not the least of which was Gabriel), then the following day, before they all left to go home. As they made their way out the door, Sloan turned to Phoebe and said, "Didn't that angel lady have pretty things?" and the cousins stared at her like she was crazy, while Phoebe privately had a heart attack.

The party wound down right after that, and the girls and Gee all helped Sheila and the caterers hustle to clean up. It all went rather quickly with so many people helping. They put out cookies and milk for Santa and carrots for the reindeer, and Gee read them the world's fastest rendition of "'Twas the Night Before Christmas." Then they put the little baby Jesus figurine in the manger in the crèche, traded the gold star Phoebe had bought for the new angel on top of the tree, and Gee shooed the girls up to bed so she could get organized for the next day.

Everyone dropped quickly off to sleep; even Gabriel, who'd had his best Christmas ever.

CHAPTER TWENTY-FOUR

Christmas

Christmas Day was a little warmer than Phoebe would have liked, and it would've been better if Gabriel hadn't broken into the living room and ripped all the wrapping paper off everyone's presents. Also, she would've liked to have had one more thing to give Gee and Sheila. But it was still her best Christmas ever.

Neeve and Kate had taken Gabriel into the kitchen while Hillary distracted Phoebe, and then they returned, releasing him back into the room with a big red bow around his neck. "Thanks, guys!" cried Phoebe, and Gee took a picture.

Besides the dog, Gee had gone totally overboard with presents. All of the girls got a beautifully framed photo of the four of them the day they planted the flag last summer. In their stocking was their favorite penny candy, and a silver link bracelet with a gull charm. There was a tiny can of blackboard paint and a paintbrush, for them to make their own blackboard at home, just like the one down in the Dorm. Each girl also got a little leather-bound Bible and a book of poems, and a tiny flask of perfume from Nate Spangleman that was called "Privet" and smelled just like the dark green hedge around the Dorm that bloomed in late June every summer. Everyone also got a gift certificate to each of their favorite stores (Summer Reading, Old Mill, Booker's, and Gullboutique), and Phoebe's eyes widened at the amount. "Wow, Gee. I don't know if even *I* will be able to spend this much there."

Gee smiled. "That's fine. You can just save the credit for when you come back next summer."

And finally, Gee gave each of them an heirloom, beautifully wrapped, with a long letter accompanying each one. For Hillary, there were three leather-bound photo albums filled with photos culled from the family collection. For Neeve, a framed antique deed to The Sound and an old, beautifully drawn map of Gull Island in a smaller, different frame. For Kate, there was the Sheehan and Callahan families' combined recipe box, and for Phoebe, an archived copy of all of the photo Christmas cards she'd ever sent of her children, plus a small trunk of vintage holiday decorations — one of each of the things the girls had used to decorate the living room, and more.

There was no way to thank Gee for her largesse, especially for the heirlooms. The girls exchanged their own gifts quietly, and adding things to the huge pile Gee had bought for Sheila (who was sleeping late today at Gee's insistence). Neeve had given Phoebe red woolen mittens — just like Laura Ingalls got in *Little House in the Big Woods* — although Neeve was quick to point out that she hadn't made them. Phoebe thanked her profusely anyway; she was touched by the gesture and grateful.

They went to church of course, and Phoebe drank it all in, her eyes tearing yet again at the beautiful carols. *I'm becoming a total sentimentalist,* thought Phoebe in dry amusement. *Either that or a crybaby.* She even hugged Gee and the cousins during the part of the mass where you were supposed to shake hands with the person next to you. Her tight squeezes prompted looks of surprise from everyone but Gee, who understood that something in Phoebe had softened and shifted in the past week.

When they got home, they ate party leftovers and took a walk on the beach, the wind blowing so hard that tears leaked from the corners of their eyes and their hair whipped their faces. Walking backward against the onslaught, Phoebe spied a crab scuttling from one pile of seaweed to another. She grabbed him before Gabriel did and held him carefully aloft in the air.

"Who's up for a crab race?" she cried into the wind.

"We all are!" Neeve cried back.

"Yeah. Cousins forever!" yelled Hillary.

"Cousins forever!" they all replied.

Meet

The Callahan Cousins

Do you have a favorite Callahan cousin?
Are you dying to know more about her?
Here are some vital tidbits about each of
the girls . . . some of which you might
not already know!

HILLARY MIRANDA CALLAHAN
Hometown: Boulder, Colorado

Hillary's Favorites: Downhill skiing, running, exploring, science, Merrell clogs, Sweetie Sweats, shrimp fajitas, and her golden retriever Winnie (named after Winnie the Pooh when Hillary was five).

Biggest fear: Being cut out of the Callahan cousin loop if her parents get divorced.

Find out more about Hillary in *The Callahan Cousins: Summer Begins* as Hillary leads the cousins in a quest to defend the Callahan family's honor when the girls find themselves caught up in an old rivalry involving a lost island, ancient family lore, and eccentric islanders. Will Hillary prove herself as the Callahan family hero, or will she get herself sent home?

Neeve

NEEVE ORLA CALLAHAN

Hometown: Good question! Born in Galway, Ireland, Neeve has lived in Kenya, China, and now Singapore.

Neeve's Favorites: Clothes with an ethnic twist, traveling, meeting new people, black coffee, Japanese techno music, soccer, languages (she speaks Swahili, Chinese, and French).

Biggest secret: Neeve loves traveling and living in eccentric places, but she has always secretly longed for a real place to call home. Neeve has decided this summer is the perfect opportunity to make Gull Island her home.

Find out more about Neeve in *The Callahan Cousins: Home Sweet Home.* Grandmother Gee has given the cousins permission to fix up and move into the Dorm—their very own quarters separate from the main house! But in the midst of their redecorating mania, Neeve stumbles upon a troubling family secret that she's reluctant to share even with her cousins.

Mary Katherine Callahan
Hometown: Westchester County, New York

Kate's Favorites: Cooking, needlepoint, painting, decorating, beef Wellington, preppy clothes, her gold charm bracelet, anything by Beatrix Potter, and generally feeling cozy.

Why she loves her cousins: They bring out the best in her. Kate tends to complicate things by being such a perfectionist, and she lets her fears hold her back from new experiences. Spending the summer with her cousins has shown her it's okay to be herself, but it's also okay not to be perfect.

Find out more about Kate in *The Callahan Cousins: Keeping Cool.* When the usually shy Kate launches a quest to become the "cool" girl in town, her over-the-top antics threaten to pull the cousins apart. Will the new Kate rule the day, or will the cousins save her before it's too late?

Phoebe

PHOEBE ANNE CALLAHAN
Hometown: Winter Park, Florida

Phoebe's Favorites: Reading (books, newspapers, magazines, etc.), hippie clothes, Swedish meatballs, Diet Coke, tennis, her leather-bound dictionary, and Uni-ball pens (because they make her handwriting look really good).

What she doesn't want her cousins to know: She worships her big sister, Daphne.

Find out more about Phoebe in *The Callahan Cousins: Together Again*. When the cousins reunite to spend Christmas vacation with Gee on Gull Island, Phoebe's plans for a perfect holiday nearly prevent her from having fun at all.

Liz Carey is a former children's book editor. She lives in New York City with her husband and three young sons, and she has twenty-five first cousins of her own. She maintains a Web site at www.thecallahancousins.com.